Hearts Key

Marianne Evans

Laura~
God Bless &
enjoy the journy!

Marian Evans

Dedication

To those who share ministry, and talent, via the wonderful Christian music I listen to each day. I'm a fan, and I'm grateful. Also, to high school sweethearts everywhere who still remember that first flush of love—and longing.

Titles by Marianne Evans

Hearts Crossing
Hearts Surrender
Hearts Communion
Hearts Key

PROLOGUE

One Year Ago

Amy Samuels shifted an armload of groceries, so she could flex her shoulder muscles. The supermarket was just a few blocks away, and she walked there whenever she could. She needed the exercise to clear her mind, and ease stress.

The front door of her home stood open; she frowned, going tense. Seeing her husband's car parked in the driveway triggered an immediate, instinctive sense of disquiet.

Mark's home. In the middle of the day. Why?

The manufacturing company he worked for was in the midst of a big job, providing parts for the next generation of SUV's. He was busy, and she didn't expect him to be home until late tonight. To be honest, Amy had been looking forward to his absence and the inner peace she knew it would bring.

Why wasn't Mark at work?

She walked inside, trying without success to ignore the sound of slamming cupboards coming from the kitchen. Wouldn't you just know it? The line of fire was exactly where she needed to deposit her stash of groceries.

All of a sudden, glassware clanged and banged, coming dangerously close to crashing. Amy steeled herself for battle.

"Mark? Mark, where's Pyper?"

His answer was an unintelligible, guttural sound.

Alarms sounded in Amy's mind, making her heart pound. "Marcey from next door was sitting with her while I shopped. What happened to Marcey?"

Braving it up, Amy crossed through the living room, taking stock. Her footsteps came to an abrupt halt. On an end table by the couch rested an open, well-sampled bottle of whiskey. Positioned right next to it she spied a tumbler, coated by dripping beads of condensation. Inside the glass were traces of gold liquid and a pool of melting ice. *So,* Amy seethed, *Mark had come home, and imbibed in the hard stuff. Nice.*

She wilted, but continued on to the kitchen. How long had the booze been out in the open? They had a rule about no whiskey in the house. What was a bottle of high-proof alcohol doing within potential reach of their four-year-old daughter?

In that instant a flashpoint occurred. Resignation and sadness morphed into rage. His reckless disregard for the safety of their daughter added fuel to her mood. "Mark!"

Mark Samuels stepped into the threshold, planting his feet firmly while he braced against the archway between the living room and kitchen. He wobbled a bit, but the stance said it all: drunken belligerence. "Back off on the sanctimonious vocals, Amy! I'm not in the mood! I'm not taking any of your crap! I mean it!"

She was so used to this. Instance by instance, Amy became immune to his menacing tone; it bore no impact or dissuasion. Calmly she moved past him and set her groceries aside on the small kitchen table. Then, she returned to the living room and picked up the bottle and glass. The new food could sit and rot for all she cared. Amy pushed past him on her way back to the kitchen where she planned to dispose of both the whiskey and the glass.

"Back off?" She stepped up to the sink but turned to glower at her husband. "Back off when you're home early from work, guzzling liquor? Where's my daughter?"

"*Our* daughter," he amended harshly, "is in her room. She's being punished. She wasn't listening and refused to do what I told her to do, so I sent her to her room until dinner."

Amy stopped short. Dinner wouldn't be ready for a couple of hours. On this humid, stifling summer day, being jailed in her room would be terrible for Pyper. Their home wasn't air conditioned, and there wouldn't be much for the four-year-old to do. Toys, games, and furnishings were sparse. In fact, it was a miracle they maintained possession of their home, considering the heavy debt load they carried and Mark's sporadic income.

She became aware once more of the bottle and glass she held. "After I toss this out, I'm telling her she's free to leave her room."

"Oh, no you're not." Mark swore liberally as he stalked in close. Looking him straight in the eye, Amy poured the remaining whiskey down the drain and threw the glass into the sink so hard it shattered.

"I see. So you think *that's* how it is." Vindictiveness shone in Marks' eyes. "That's just *fine*."

He staggered to the small china hutch tucked into a corner of the kitchen. Crafted of maple, it was well worn, a beloved heirloom from Amy's grandmother. They had inherited the piece a couple years ago. Mark yanked open the doors. With sloppy motions he reached inside. He grabbed stacks of dishes from inside and just let them fall.

Irreplaceable, depression-era glass and Rosenthal china smashed to the floor. "We even yet? Want s'more?"

Amy ran, pulling on Mark's arm in an attempt to get him away from the cabinet. But he was a big man, solid muscle; when she came near, he shook her off easily, sending her to the floor in a sprawl. She righted herself quickly, stumbling against the refrigerator.

"Stop it! Stop! *Please* stop!" Helpless, she could do nothing but watch while Mark swiped at an artfully arranged display of wine goblets. Soon they were reduced to nothing more than sparkling shards that decorated the hardwood floor.

Amy cried out, thinking of the beautiful memories held within those few precious mementos from her past: the family dinners, holiday celebrations, happy laughter. Her china was sacrosanct, one of the few things she refused to pawn in order to support her family.

The china and…

Mark spied her camera, a simple digital unit that was her lifeline to sanity. A part of what augmented her income as a receptionist for a fitness center in Sterling Heights, Michigan. Her heart lurched. *No*, she screamed in silence. *Please, no! I have a freelance assignment this weekend!*

The inner plea came just seconds too late.

He hefted the small, silver unit, which gleamed and still looked like new even two years after purchase because Amy pampered and cared for it. Photography was her release, her joy…and Mark was about to destroy it!

He threw the camera against the wall; it burst apart on impact and Amy cried out, sinking against the counter.

"I got fire—laid off today." He continued to storm through the kitchen. "Stupid idiots in charge of that stinkin' factory don't know their left hand from their right." He spun toward her. "So if you push me now, I'll push you right back. If you get in my way, I'll take you right out of it!"

Amy didn't doubt that fact for a minute. However, she hadn't missed the slipup Mark made between being fired and being laid off. Her husband was defeating himself. Again. He was taking her right down with him. Again. Gambling, booze, and spotty work attendance had combined to do him in. Again. Amy scraped the very bottom of her heart, trying desperately to find even the tiniest piece of hope for her relationship with Mark. The effort was answered only in an emptiness that stole her joy, and ever increasing fears for herself and Pyper.

She wished for surcease, but all the wishing in the world wouldn't make the nightmare of living with Mark go away. Not this time. Amy knew she alone had the power to make a final move and end this abuse and insane pattern of living—not just for her sake, but for Pyper's as well.

Mark ranted on. "I lose my job, and I'm not gonna be able to get another one any time soon living in this Godforsaken place." Amy winced at his curse. Although she no longer attended church regularly, like she used to—back in happier, more innocent times—the use of God's name in vain scalded a place in her spirit and returned her to who, and what, she used to be.

He kept on raging. "I don't want griping from you, Amy. If I want a drink after work, not you or anyone else is gonna stop me! You have a choice. Clean up this mess and deal with it, or get out of my sight!"

Frozen with terror, Amy stared as he kicked furniture, trashed cupboards, and systematically destroyed the kitchen. Then, something in her mind snapped. She couldn't hold back the cry of angry frustration that bubbled up from her chest. Now, every-day dishes joined the pile of chaos. She barely dodged being hit by the plate her husband threw.

This is insanity, she thought. *No one should have to live this way.*

"If it weren't for your drinking and gambling, we might make it! If you'd discipline yourself to live a normal life, you'd be able to function at work and keep a job! Instead you'd rather hock everything we own, right down to your soul, for a night of poker, or a night of drinking so you can go numb!" She pulled him away from the cupboard; anger-driven adrenaline made her strong. "It's easier that way, isn't it? Well not for me! I'm sick of it! I'm sick of being trashed— literally and emotionally! I'm sick of living in debt! I'm sick of being heartbroken! Most of all I'm sick to death and tired of not giving Pyper the life she deserves. You need *help*—"

"Get out!" Mark pounced on her like a rabid animal, shoving her against the kitchen counter so hard that an explosion of pain shot up her back and spine, and she lost her breath. An instant later, the back of his hand crossed her face with such impact she saw red haze and had to fight off nausea. "I said *get out*!"

Amy refused to give in. For Pyper's sake, she had

to persevere. She squirmed away from his grasp. This marriage was finished. With that realization came a degree of resolution that lent her additional strength.

"Fine. I'll leave. But not without my daughter. She is *not* staying with you."

In that instant, all the anger left his face. She watched as her words sank in. Only then did Amy realize her mistake. She had exposed her greatest vulnerability. Pyper. Mark remained just lucid enough to connect the emotional dots and play an ace.

"Get out of here if that's what you want—but you don't get Pyper. She's *mine*."

Her heart endured a shower of spears. How could she possibly leave without Pyper? She had to get to her daughter! Amy would never, ever leave without her.

She stared at her husband, her vision blurred by tears. She had to find a way to Pyper. Backing slowly away, she noticed the way he moved toward her, bullying her into the living room. He wore a gloating expression, moving her slowly, and inexorably, to the front door.

"Go ahead. Just try to get her. *Try* it."

He deliberately blocked the hallway that led to the two bedrooms of their home. Amy could hear Pyper crying now, and that left her frantic. She wanted to scream—crumple up and wail.

God, please, please, give me strength! Send me help!

There came no instant answer, no miraculous flash.

"My things," she objected weakly. Her belongings were all she could think of that might get her past him and into the hallway of rooms to grab Pyper.

Mark stood solid, his posture unyielding. He advanced her a few more steps toward the front door, and away from Pyper. "Get 'em later. If they're still around."

Finally, as though he could tolerate her no longer, Mark shoved her onto the front porch and slammed the door shut. The dead bolt banged into place with added emphasis. Panic swept through her body and quickly overwhelmed. She had no purse. No keys. No cell phone. No money. She had nothing but the shorts, t-shirt and tennis shoes she wore.

And she didn't have Pyper.

Desperate, her breath exiting in a heaving, labored effort, Amy looked toward the front windows of the house. Fear kept her from thinking clearly, yet she had to figure out a way to get Pyper away from Mark.

Not giving herself time to reconsider, she climbed through a hedge of thigh-high evergreen shrubs that surrounded their house. Her clothes were no protection against the long, stabbing needles. The window to Pyper's bedroom was open. The sound of her daughter moving around inside only increased her obsession to get her free as she worked her way through the bushes as quietly and as quickly as possible.

Standing on tiptoe, Amy looked inside. The expression of bleak, hopeless fear on Pyper's face prodded her on.

"Pyper…Pyper Marie…" She didn't want to speak too loud for fear of alerting Mark. "Come to the window, sweetheart. It's OK. Come here to Mama."

Shaking, her wide eyes brimming with tears, Pyper inched her way to the window. "Mama, get me! I scared! Get me now! *Please!*"

Fat tears rolled down Pyper's plump, red cheeks. A thick, curling tumble of blonde hair fell to her waist.

Dressed in a tank top, shorts and flip-flops, the vision of her daughter consumed Amy, and spurred her on.

"Hush, baby! Hush! I'm not leaving you! I'm not going anywhere without you." Scanning the window line, Amy thought out loud. "I've got to open the screen." There wasn't much a four-year-old could do to help, but as she spoke, Amy spotted a tiny hole in the netting of the screen that she might be able to use to pry the screen off and pull it free. She worked fast, jimmying the protective cover relentlessly, making the tear larger and larger.

Soon she ripped away the piece of finely-woven metal.

Sweat beaded her face. Nerve-inspired heat nearly sent her world into a tailspin. But in that instant, Pyper reached out for her, and Amy grabbed onto her for all she was worth. Her control firmly in check, Amy dragged Pyper through the window.

Freedom. Blessed, precious freedom. But for how long?

They ran down the street and headed toward a nearby convenience store. The life she chose with Mark had left Amy alienated from her family, from friends, and everyone else she had held dear just five short years ago. The only thing she knew she could do now was place a collect phone call to the most welcoming place she had ever known, and fall into the arms of a God she hardly believed in any longer.

As she prayed a prodigal might return to the sanctuary of Woodland Church, she dialed operator assistance. "Please tell Pastor Ken Lucerne that this is a collect call, from Amy Maxwell," she said when the woman came on the line. Her voice shook. She knew Pastor Ken wouldn't recognize her married name of

Samuels. Everyone at Woodland had known her as Amy Maxwell—the bubbly and sparkling life of the party, the leader of the youth group. Once upon a time, she'd been the girl most likely to succeed and take the world by storm.

Oh, how far I've fallen, she thought on a choking sob.

The call rang through and she waited, tightly clutching Pyper, praying insane, ridiculous prayers of promise and petition that Mark wouldn't spot her. That safety might be hers and Pyper's once more. Somehow. Some way.

"Ken Lucerne," came a warm, deep voice.

Amy nearly went faint with relief while the operator informed him of the collect call. She clung tight to Pyper; she clung tight to the edge of the plastic encasement of the public phone, cradling the receiver against her shoulder. Tears fell free, and she trembled.

"Yes, I'll accept the charges." The operator clicked off and Ken took it from there. "Amy, honey, what's the matter? Are you OK?"

She could barely talk she was shaking so bad. His tender concern allowed her the luxury of a complete, and much-needed internal collapse. "Pastor Ken, can you please…can you help me? I'm in such a huge mess, and you're the only one I could think of to help. I'm so sorry to bother you, I just…I…"

"Where are you?"

She didn't answer the question. "I don't know how long I can stay here. He might find me, and Pyper, and that'll be the end…of everything! I—"

"Sweetheart, rest easy. Where are you? I'll come get you." Though he interrupted, his voice was so reassuring. A calm in the storm.

"I'm at Robtell's Quick Mart on Groesbeck."

There was the slightest of pauses. "I can be there in ten minutes, fifteen tops. Are you in any kind of danger?"

"I just don't know anymore, Pastor Ken. I don't know anything right now. All I know is I'm scared! I need help!"

"Stay right there, Amy. I'm on my way."

Ken hung up abruptly, and she found she could actually breathe again. Pyper clung to her neck, burying her face in Amy's neck, shaking with tears. "Baby, I'm so, so sorry for putting you through this." She pushed through the doorway to the store. It was cool inside; that helped. There was also a deep, empty window ledge where Amy sank down and waited in an obscurity she embraced. Slowly she uncoiled, knowing she would need some aspirin for the pain that echoed through her back and her face. She rested her head against the cool plate glass and drew in deep, steadying breaths.

It's over, Mark. From this day on you are no longer a part of our lives, and neither is this horrible, sickening fear. Not once after this nightmare passes will I allow myself to look back.

1

Present Day

"Mr. Brock, we're pulling in at Woodland. You all set? Ready to go?"

"And then some." Tyler Brock moved to a nearby window next to Anthony, their driver. "Hey, Anthony? How long have we been on tour together?"

"Almost three years, sir. Why?"

Even as they spoke, the enormous tour bus swung into the parking lot of Woodland Church. The first landmark of Tyler's arrival home was the familiar, beautiful brick bell tower, topped by a gleaming, simple cross. The sight filled him with warmth. He smiled. Opposite the church crested the pristine, diamond-tipped waters of Lake Saint Clair.

"Well I'm just wonderin'. D'you think it might be possible for you to call me Tyler?"

Anthony chuckled. "No, sir. Sorry."

"Glad we got that settled." Tyler spared him a wry look.

The chauffer shook his head and grinned. "Likewise, Mr. Brock."

Theirs was an age-old back and forth. Tyler gave up the battle and instead looked outside the rectangular window as Anthony navigated the vehicle to a slow, shimmying stop. Tyler took note of familiar surroundings. Michigan. Saint Clair Shores. Woodland Church. *Home.*

He really had been gone too long.

Excitement filled him, dancing across his nerve endings like a live wire. A crowd of people converged on the bus and the equipment semi that followed close behind.

The first face he saw belonged to Ken Lucerne. The pastor of Woodland Church stood at the front of the gathering of about a hundred or so people. Rimming the crowd were members of the local news media. Kiara, Ken's wife, stood next to him. The happiness that expanded in Tyler's chest increased.

He knew the drill. He had lived it repeatedly over the last four, almost five, years. But never here. Never at the heart of where he had been raised, and never at Woodland, his faith-home since birth.

He prepared to exit the bus. "Thanks for the smooth ride, Tony. As ever."

"Pleasure, as ever. Have a great concert, Mr. Brock."

In passing, before he trotted down the bus steps, Tyler gave Tony's shoulder an affectionate clap, and they traded nods. The rest of his team—both musical and technical—gathered up and prepared to walk out with him.

The doors whooshed open, unfolding into a world of smiling faces, camera lights, cheers, colorful poster-board signs, and desperate calls for his attention. The instant his feet hit the asphalt, the focus was on him, and it was chaos.

"Tyler! Tyler we love you!"

"Tyler, over here, please."

"Can you look this way?"

"How does it feel to be back in Michigan?"

"How long will you be here?"

"Tyler! Can we have an autograph? Please?"

"Can you comment on the addition of a second show tomorrow night, since this one sold out in hours?"

Tyler walked smoothly through the din—the strobes of cameras, the video floodlights, the shouts and jostling. He went straight to Pastor Ken, his mentor in so many ways. He had to weave through clusters of young ladies who carried glitter-covered signs, and wore bright, hopeful smiles. He had to dodge a few other bodies along the way, but he made it.

Suddenly he was seventeen years old all over again—shy but eager—hoping desperately to take on the world, and his dreams...

"Hey, Pastor Ken." Tyler found himself instantly enfolded in a hug that he returned with equal force and conviction.

"It's so good to see you again, son."

Tyler didn't allow the hubbub to decrease meaning. He paused to look right into Ken's eyes with heartfelt emphasis. "You too. You look great."

Ken groaned in a self-deprecating manner, drawing Kiara close to his side. The gesture made Tyler feel good. They were such a great pair. A team in love and in life. "Well, there's a bit of fresh gray around the temples these days, but I blame that on our little Annie. Wait until you meet her. She's a pistol."

"And I happen to like that subtle touch of silver," Kiara said before she, too, hugged Tyler close. "I've missed you!"

A spring breeze, sweetened by an undercurrent of

fresh flowers, lifted Kiara's long, straight hair. She gave Tyler a smile sparkling with delight and so beautiful—just like her. "How are you doing with the youth group?" he asked. "I hear you're the director now."

"Great…and we're growing! I love it. In fact, about twenty members are waiting inside for the meet and greet. You good with that?"

"Absolutely. Lead the way."

"We figured the kids would appreciate that you were such a vital part of Woodland's youth ministry years ago," Ken continued, "and give the S.T.A.G.E. group some added impact. After the meet and greet, you'll have time for a sound check, and a bite to eat before the concert."

"Perfect."

S.T.A.G.E. The acronym for Woodland's youth group left Tyler swept through by nostalgia. *Super Teen Angels Go Evangelize.* By God's grace alone, he had been given the opportunity to heed that call. As they moved toward Woodland's activity center, Tyler paused, signing CD covers, photos, and posters for whoever happened to be closest.

"Today and tonight are crazy." Ken gave Tyler a look that bordered on apologetic. "I promise tomorrow will be much quieter. Dinner, at our place, with you and your family. If you're game."

"You better believe it. Thanks!"

"Do you ever get used to this…this…frenzy?" Kiara viewed the assemblage with wide, disbelieving eyes.

Before answering, Tyler paused just long enough for a quick photo-op with a doe-eyed fan who wore an earnest, dazzled expression.

"Sort of, but never completely." He lifted a

shoulder. "What matters most is the fact that I get to share my music, and my own kind of ministry. That's all I ever wanted."

"I remember." The corner of Kiara's mouth curved. She arched a brow. Tyler didn't need a roadmap to recognize that her thoughts had gone back in time, to a mission trip to Pennsylvania during which they had all grown to know, and love, one another.

He remembered as well. That's why—despite Ken and Kiara, despite the media frenzy and solid press of fans—Tyler searched for one face. One person. Despite the five years that had gone by, there was no way he'd miss the one he sought. None at all.

Amy Maxwell.

Would she be here? Was she even still around the Shores? What was she doing now? He was too shy to be obvious about his interest and ask. Ken would have unlocked the answers to those questions better than anyone else. A more active, engaged pastor Tyler had never come across in his life.

But he wanted the matters of his heart to unfold on their own. He trusted God to reveal her—or not—according to His intent.

Nonetheless, Tyler couldn't help hoping. Was she the same compelling, beautiful girl of his memory? He really hoped God's will was to have their paths intersect once more. In large part, she was the reason why he had come back to Woodland in the first place.

"We've only got about an hour and a half for the meet and greet," Ken said. "We've given everyone the rules, but once these kids see you, the excitement is going to be difficult to contain. They're going to be all over you. Timetables might fly out the window."

"No worries, I'm used to it. It'll be OK. If we have

to shorten the sound check to make sure everyone is taken care of, that's not a huge deal. The tech crew is setting up as we speak, and they're the best. They know what they're doing."

Inside the activity center, multi-colored streamers, balloons, and music notes in shimmering silver and gold foil hung from the ceiling. A couple dozen teens and their parents milled about—after completing a meal, judging by the used plastic dishware on the tables and stuffed into trashcans. Others sat on metal folding chairs surrounding long, tables.

Spontaneous applause erupted, along with a chorus of cheers and greetings. Tyler waved and walked toward a podium at the far end of the room. A sense of honor and awe worked through him. It never failed to humble Tyler that the message, and impact, of his music ignited this kind of response, this kind of loyalty and affection.

"Hey, everybody! Thanks… thanks." He waited for the noise to diminish. "I appreciate you coming out tonight." He gestured both to stem the additional applause and to encourage folks to return to their seats. "Of course I want you to know how much I appreciate your support of the new album, and your encouragement. It truly does keep me, and the rest of my team, motivated to do our best both for you, and for the glory of the God we serve."

Applause broke out once again. While Tyler waited, he scanned the room, taking in faces and smiles and affection. A doorway at the rear of the room came open just far enough to admit a stealthy, sheepish-looking newcomer.

Tallish, and slender—almost too slender—she entered the room. Long, blonde hair fashioned into a utilitarian braid, trailed in a thick line down her back. Large, blue eyes, more guarded, a bit more tired than he recalled, completed the picture. A white Oxford shirt, sleeves rolled up to her elbows, revealed petite arms. Tucked into a pair of low-slung blue jeans cinched by a thick leather belt, the shirt modestly accentuated a shapely figure. She slid the neck strap of her camera into place as she took a fast sweep of the room.

She looked right at him and Tyler's throat went dry. It only took a heartbeat, a breath really, and Amy Maxwell reentered his life.

But the hesitance he detected was shocking. The Amy Maxwell who lived in the memories of his heart was the epitome of self-assurance and spunk.

Just one thing kept him from stumbling: a hard-won sense of perseverance and smooth polish. "Beyond the music, beyond any kind of acclaim people might offer, I consider this a ministry. My music is something I feel honor-bound to share with believers and non-believers alike in a spirit of love, hope, and faith. Look at tonight, for example. The good works you're supporting through the Macomb County Shelter are for the benefit of everyone—no matter what their situation, life circumstance, or faith. I'm proud to be just a small part of that endeavor, and support Woodland Church as we do our best to bring Christ to the world. Thanks for joining me on this journey, folks. I hope you enjoy the concert, and I'm looking forward to meeting you one-on-one."

The concluding words shot a circuit of electricity through the orderly, but expectant, assembly. Tyler, meanwhile, barely managed to cohesively finish his introductory speech.

Amy kept her distance. She tucked into a corner and alternated between fiddling nervously with her camera and stealing glances at him every now and again. How odd was that? How come the bubbly, take-charge girl he remembered from high school now acted like a timid fan? The irony of such a thing almost made him laugh out loud. Tables surely hadn't turned *that* much. Sure, he was building a career as a Christian music artist, but just one look at Amy Maxwell and he instantly fell back to the days of being a shy, gangly boy who wanted nothing more than to spend time with the sweetest, and most popular girl at Saint Clair Shores High School.

A growing press of people forced Tyler to snap to proper attention. Meet-and-greets were one of his favorite parts of being on tour, but this hour-long window of sharing with his fans tended to be fast-paced and excluded any focus but the people who came up to meet him. In many instances, they had waited hours to simply shake his hand, or get a picture, or an autograph. As such, Tyler refused to shortchange a single soul.

After all, Amy was here—with a camera, no less. That didn't surprise him much. She had been the official photographer on the mission trip to Pennsylvania years ago. And now, she was headed his way.

Still, she approached slowly. She didn't make direct eye contact for any appreciable amount of time. Instead, she focused on Ken and Kiara who stood nearby and ushered the group into a reception line.

Just like in high school, Tyler's heart reacted to Amy's presence by skipping into an impassioned form of overdrive. Just like in high school, he experienced that bittersweet yearning for a woman who captivated him...yearning, and that inexhaustible heat of longing.

But the nearer she moved, the more Tyler realized she didn't just *act* different, she *looked* different, too—as though she carried an enormous weight. Oh, she was as beautiful as ever, and her eyes, when she dared look his way, seemed as clear and as vibrant a shade of blue as he remembered, but she seemed drained. Her posture and movements, formerly brimming with confidence, now spoke of being browbeaten and cautious in the extreme.

Sad.

Something had robbed Amy of the joyful spirit she had possessed, the spirit that had drawn in, and touched, everyone who came into contact with her. To so deeply impact a person of such strength, it had to have been something harsh. She looked like a changed woman.

Why?

2

Now more than ever Amy sought refuge behind the filter of a camera lens. Viewing the world from the safety of a photographer's eye created distance, an emotional and physical buffer that enabled her to create the pictures of her heart often without having to engage in the deeper aspects of what she saw and cataloged. Far safer that way, she knew. Far less a chance of getting hurt.

That is, until the moment she walked into the Woodland Church Activity Center and began her commission as the evening's photographer.

"Amazing," she murmured, dazzled somewhat by the atmosphere, but even more so by the man who stood at the center of the festivities.

Tyler Brock had come a long way since the last time she'd seen him. He was now a polished, confident man. That recognition hit Amy right between the curves of her tender, broken heart and set butterflies free.

Instant infatuation. She knew the symptoms, and infatuation was the last thing she needed. Additionally, infatuation with an acclaimed Christian music star? *Yeah.* Like every other woman on the planet.

For now, she needed to release past history and get to work. She was here for the youth group members who had been given the opportunity to meet Tyler Brock, nothing more.

When Amy walked up, Kiara waved to garner everyone's attention. "Before we begin, let me take you through the way things will work. First of all, you're in line, by family, to have an opportunity to share a few words with Tyler, get an autograph, and a picture." Kiara turned to Amy.

Amy took a nerve-stilling breath, which didn't work in the least toward calming her nerves.

Kiara smiled and gave a nod. "In an effort to give you each the most time allowed with Tyler and to keep the line moving forward at a fair pace for everyone else, no cameras are allowed. Instead, to capture the moment, Amy Matthews will be taking pictures for you, and they'll be posted tomorrow morning on the Woodland Church website where you'll be able to download them for free."

Ken stepped up to the table where Tyler stood and handed him a can of pop. Sure enough, it was Vernors. She remembered how much Tyler loved the Michigan-made ginger ale.

Tyler sat casually on the edge of the table, his legs dangling while he watched and waited. After popping the lid of the can and downing a long sip, he settled the beverage next to him. The vision of this more developed version of the high school friend she had cared for, was dramatic.

"Amy and Tyler have the common history of being members of STAGE, just like you. In fact, they attended a mission trip to Pennsylvania years ago. They know and understand where you're coming from, because they've both been there."

"You used to hang out with Tyler?" the first girl in

line piped up. "Boy, are you lucky."

Amy blushed and Tyler laughed while Ken and Kiara gracefully covered that ebullient comment. There was no chance to speak with Tyler directly, of course, so instead she focused on her mental walk-through of who Tyler had once been versus the man he had become.

To say Tyler Brock had come of age, to say he had outgrown the cocoon of quiet, gawky but straightforward teenager, was gross understatement.

Kiara gave Amy a nod, letting her know her job had begun. Camera at the ready, Amy stepped up and began framing shots, clicking away while Tyler welcomed his fans. He filled her lens, in more than just a literal way. Tyler was sculpted beautifully, and handsome. He wore his hair just a touch long in back, but combed away from his face in well-styled waves of light brown. Jeans and an un-tucked, deep green shirt emphasized his hazel eyes.

Which were presently focused on her.

Or, her camera, to be more precise. Amy broke loose from her thoughts and realized the family standing near Tyler waited on her. She executed a nicely framed shot of them as they concluded their visit with Tyler.

When she lowered her camera, Tyler's attention remained fixed on her, and he gave her a private, quirked smile. Amy felt the power of it clear down to the farthest, most aching regions of her heart. She lowered her gaze and sighed, double-checking her equipment, fiddling unnecessarily with calibrations. The past came calling once more, eating away at her resolve to think of nothing else but her photography duties.

Once upon a time, Tyler had perched his heart on his sleeve, with an arrow that pointed straight at her. Meanwhile, she had taken him in as a friend, with authentic care, yet blithely took him for granted. Now, times and tables hadn't just turned between them, they had spun wildly out of control.

In response to that recognition, Amy steeled her spine and became resolute, lifting her camera with newfound determination to move past emotional folly. The next group stepped forward. Throughout the remainder of the greeting session, she melted to the sidelines, tucked away by design from direct interactions.

I'm not being a coward, she told herself. *I'm not letting this whole unsettling reunion thing set me off balance. I'm simply being unobtrusive, like any good photographer.*

Still, one truth remained in place, no matter what her rebuttals. The camera remained her guard. It opened up a wonderful opportunity to focus on Tyler and re-familiarize herself with him, yet at the same time, kept her safely distant and protected. The best of both worlds.

෨∞ఞ

Woodland Church featured two-tier seating, and an altar that was raised a step. There, tour crews had set up overhead lights, sound equipment, and instruments. The concert kicked off without a hitch.

Amy continued to chronicle Tyler's visit, moving fluidly through the venue to capture a variety of shots: crowd responses, multi-colored lights playing across surfaces of the stage, the faces of the audience, Tyler and his band.

Whenever she paused to take in the scene and view the world around her in the context of a potential photograph, a twitch of loss and unpleasant emotion speared her heart—especially when Tyler interacted with his back-up singers.

And then he introduced his duet partner, Rebecca Graham—brought her center stage and kissed her cheek. They shared on on-stage sass and connection that was eloquent. It Amy froze in place.

Rebecca's sparkling, genuine smile, her easy grace and charm on stage—particularly with Tyler—sent a bead of regret across Amy's skin. She could have had that with Tyler. Camaraderie. Companionship. Instead, she'd let him go.

Tyler and Rebecca drew up stools and placed them side-by-side. The spotlight tunneled in and focused on the two of them alone while the rest of the houselights went dim.

Amy fell into the scene, her camera forgotten.

Microphone in hand and at the ready, Rebecca perched gracefully on her stool, her lace skirt of peach and her sparkling tank top accentuated by a gauzy over-shirt of stark white. Fiery red hair shimmered in wavy curls that fell to her shoulders. She slid it aside while she waited. That's when Amy fell victim to a nasty shock. An unpleasant stab agitated her already prickly nervous system. The taut sense of disquiet she fought? It wasn't just regret. It stemmed from jealousy. Plain and simple. This was a gorgeous woman who spent long hours at Tyler's side, and that bugged Amy.

As if that reaction made any degree of sense.

Meanwhile, Rebecca waited, as appealing as an angel, watching Tyler as his fingers strummed an acoustic guitar in a melody that began to take shape.

"I want to tell you the story of Amazing Grace," he said quietly, in a hushed, moving tone that held the entire crowed enthralled. "Now, I'm not talking about the traditional, time-honored hymn we all love." Music rolled through the church, slow and haunting. "Rather, this is the story of a woman. A woman named Grace. What makes her amazing? Her journey of faith. Amazing Grace travels the badlands spoken of so eloquently in Psalm 23, but through love, and the grace of God, she emerges on the other side. She's amazing because she never gives up on her faith, on her God. Therein she finds her hope. Her redemption. Her *grace.*"

The song began in earnest—a stirring duet that emphasized just how skilled, and syncopated, Tyler and Rebecca were as performers.

Or perhaps even more.

Trembling, trying to maintain focus, and distance, Amy lifted her camera, but she just couldn't click the shutter. She nipped at the inside of her cheek and lowered the lens. Tears stung her eyes as the words of the song—of heartache, surrender to pain, a renewal of faith, hope and love—took root in her heart and left her moved yet so desperately at a loss in her own life.

The audience was captivated, strung together on pearls of music and harmony. Words and notes drew them in. Moments later, Amazing Grace concluded— pitch perfect and on a blended note that echoed through the facility for long moments afterward. Following an awed silence, applause erupted; the crowd moved to its feet in unison.

Tyler joined hands with Rebecca and lifted them high, turning toward her to give her a moment in the spotlight. He kissed the back of her hand and they shared a telling look before separating. When moisture spattered against the top of her camera, Amy came abruptly alert and steeled her emotions. She brushed away her tears, giving herself a hard internal shake.

That's when a gentle nudge came from behind. Then an arm slid around her waist. "You OK, Amy?" Pastor Ken asked.

She took a deep breath, but the effort ended on a none-too-graceful hiccup. She cleared her throat to cover that display of weakness. "I'm OK."

"Kiara noticed your reaction. She wanted me to lend some support if you need it."

Amy's shoulders relaxed a bit beneath the strength of his hold. She hung her head and fingered her camera. Ken and Kiara were two of the most gentle-hearted, caring people she had ever known. They had taken her in for a time and helped her land on her feet. Thank God.

"I'll be fine…the song just hit me."

"And Tyler's hitting you, too?" There was a trace of knowing in his tone. "I remember the connection you two shared back when."

"In different times, yes. He was always a great friend." Amy lifted her chin and found just enough steady resolve to reply with a bit of her former spirit and pluck. "He's doing great, isn't he? I'm really proud of him."

"You know what? You should tell him that. I'm sure he'd appreciate it."

Amy shrugged casually, but realized she had walked right into that one.

"Do it tomorrow at dinner. We'd love to have you and Pyper join us for a small get-together Kiara and I are hosting to welcome him home. Can you make it?"

Amy's gaze lobbed from the stage, to Ken, to Kiara, back to Tyler, then Rebecca.

Torture. Dinner with Tyler and the crew would only serve to magnify the chasm between her life and his. The changes. Further attempts at a connection would only end up breaking her heart, and increase awareness of everything her life lacked—and all it could have been under different, and better-chosen, circumstances.

"I'll think about it." Amy gave him a wan smile and lifted her camera once again. She started taking pictures, and Ken moved slowly away, but she could tell she remained on his radar screen. And Kiara's.

That was a blessing, and a burden. She hated the idea of others continually having to mentor her, care for her, and feel compelled to intervene. But by the same token? Thank *God* they were there, and in her corner. And Pyper's as well.

ॐॐ

When the concert ended, a few authorized guests and Woodland VIP's gathered in a cordoned off area for a backstage visit at the activity center. Then and there Amy decided it was time to give Tyler a proper greeting. After all, her emotional issues were hers alone. At a minimum she owed their past a gesture of support.

The noise level was intimidating as a celebration of the show kicked off, but it didn't take long for Amy to find Tyler; the crowd ebbed and flowed around him like a tide. He stood comfortably amidst it all, his arm looped around his mom's waist, his father nearby as well. The image made Amy smile. Mr. and Mrs. Brock radiated familial pride, and judging by the way she kept her sparkling eyes and happy smile trained upon her son, Mrs. Brock—LuAnne, Amy recalled—was delighted to have Tyler back home again, if only for a couple of days. According to Ken, he'd be staying with them tonight and tomorrow. Back home again.

If only it were that easy.

Amy took a deep breath. It was time to move forward, and act like the friend she had always been. She made progress toward approaching Tyler, watching as he shook hands with members of his crew and received enthusiastic hugs of support. Then in came Rebecca. He saw her immediately and grinned while she made a dash for his ready embrace. She gave a happy shout as he lifted her up, and spun her in a full circle.

"You were great," she enthused, her voice touched by the cadence of the south. "Honestly, what a show!"

"Inspired, wasn't it, Becs? It feels so good to be home!"

Rebecca pecked both his cheeks and smiled into his eyes. Amy's heart sank. His dynamic backup singer then greeted others around them and dissolved into the crowd of tour staffers. Amy winced, battling off turmoil, self-doubt, and inadequacy.

It was a battle she lost.

In that instant, her mature, straightforward intentions vaporized. Hiking up her purse and camera strap, Amy kept a tight hold on them both as she turned to leave. She took a few steps toward the exit. She'd beg off tomorrow's dinner, and bid this entire, world-rocking episode farewell. In the morning, everything would be back to normal. In the morning, she could—"Seriously?"

Amy froze at the sound of the smooth and deep voice that carried with it just a touch of the South. She closed her eyes, and she trembled. Bad.

"You were seriously gonna leave without sayin' hello to me?"

She couldn't pull in a proper breath. Her heart skittered wildly. Red-hot heat crawled up the skin of her neck and ignited her cheeks, melting and burning in one fell swoop.

Bravely she turned around, her lips pressed tight, though she fought through it all to offer a tentative smile. "Hey, Tyler."

It was the best she could manage. His eyes were unspeakably gentle and tender. His attitude of warmth so typical of the Tyler she had known, once upon a life. Amy welcomed that fact, and at the same time, she was swept away by just looking at him.

"Hey, Amy," he greeted softly. His smile bloomed when he took her hands. A beat later, he drew her in for a long, tight hug that left her aching. He felt so hard, and strong. So wonderful. A lump formed fast in her throat—a bit of mourning, she supposed, for all she missed.

"I, ah, didn't want to interfere or anything." As soon as the words crossed her lips, she realized how lame they sounded.

Tyler kissed her cheek, and Amy went a bit dizzy. A bit weak at the knees. "You couldn't interfere if you wanted to." He leaned back and drew a fingertip against her chin; he looked deep into her eyes. "I've missed you."

3

The last thing on earth Tyler wanted to do was step away from Amy, and this much-longed-for moment of reunion. Despite the tumult of activity taking place around them, he experienced the certainty of a connecting rod between them. It was as if they were isolated as a single unit despite the blur and rush of the activity center.

Just as he was ready to speak to her again, the double doors of the facility pushed open once more. A pair of little tornados, dressed in the guise of angelic-looking young girls, burst onto the scene with enough combined power to break the spell. One of them, a pixie with an ocean of long, curly blonde hair, bee-lined to Amy and grabbed her legs.

"Mommy! Mommy, I'm so excited! Annie says I get to have dinner with her tomorrow at her house, and we had fun with Miss Monica and all the other kids! We played house and we played games, and we colored pictures while you concert-ed!"

The words came out rapid-fire, bubbling with excitement. On a fast track, his mind processed the words: Mommy—that would be Amy. Annie—that would be Ken and Kiara's daughter, the one Pastor Ken had described as a pistol. Dinner—tomorrow night at Ken and Kiara's.

But his thoughts bounced back repeatedly to just

one word in that laundry list of information. *Mommy.* Amy was a mother.

Did you think she had gone into seclusion, Brock? Come on. She always possessed tremendous allure and magnetism. Remember that all-star athlete from high school she went to homecoming with right after the mission trip to Pennsy? What was his name? Samuels something. He was the 'King of the School,' and even he fell all over himself to be with Amy Maxwell. In fact, they were all but engaged when you saw the writing on the wall and chucked everything in Michigan to head south, to the only dream you had left to pursue: Music.

That brought him back around again. *Maxwell.* If she was married, why did she still go by the last name of Maxwell? Amy had always been independent, and a strong-minded person in their youth, but she hardly fit the type who'd refuse a man's name in marriage.

New realities, new questions, crashed in while Amy whisked her daughter upward with a happy exclamation then pulled her in tight, holding her in her arms as snug as a caterpillar in a cocoon. Her eyes, however, were a reflection of hesitance. "Pyper, this is Tyler Brock. He's a friend of mine, and the one who sang for everyone tonight. Can you say hello?"

Pyper was a mini-Amy. The child was shy, but possessed a sparkling personality that instantly touched his soul. Pyper leaned back against Amy, however, keeping distant from him; still, she was polite, and so sweet looking. She thrust out her little hand with formality. "Hello, Mr. Tyler."

Tyler took hold of her hand, careful not to impose himself beyond a simple grasp and squeeze. He looked into the child's sea-colored eyes and smiled widely. "Pyper, it's an honor. I'm so glad to meet you."

She didn't respond. Instead, her brows pulled together, and she remained glued to Amy, searching him thoroughly.

Tyler was undeterred. "Did I hear something about pictures you made?"

Pyper nodded, and her hair shimmered and bounced.

"I'd sure love to see them."

Silence strode in. In his periphery, he saw Amy's gaze lift to his in surprise. Meanwhile, a second bout of shyness came over Pyper. She snugged a bit closer to Amy's neck, looking at him with hesitance. Then, she leaned back and blinked at Amy. "Can Annie come, too?"

In unison, Tyler and Amy glanced toward Ken and Kiara's daughter. As expected, she stood next to her parents, chatting with Kiara while Ken conversed with members of Tyler's family.

"OK, you can go see if she wants to join us."

Pyper crawled from Amy's embrace and scrabbled for the ground. "Annie! Annie, c'mere!"

They were alone once more. People seemed to sense, and respect, his focus on Amy; therefore, he was given a bit of a berth. His heart pounded hard and fast. "Wow. Your daughter is absolutely phenomenal."

"Thanks. She warms up, but...well..."

"It takes time?"

Amy nodded. "Especially around men. I don't want you to take it personally or anything."

Especially around men? That comment begged even more questions, so did Amy's guarded, timid posture. But this was not the time or place. Instead, wanting only for her to be comfortable with him, Tyler deflected. "I'm the reformed shy-guy, as you know better than anyone else. So, I can relate."

Amy's gaze lifted to his, and Tyler saw what he wanted—a heavy downgrade in her discomfort. She even smiled. "A lack of shyness isn't the only change."

"Oh?"

She nodded. "The accent, for example."

She had always known how to catch him by surprise. She glanced at him with the sassy light in her eyes that he remembered best, the one that even now caused a pulse rush. He took in her playful expression and heat blanketed his system. "A bit of one, yeah. I suppose five years in Nashville is bound to rub off on a person. As for losing my shyness, well, life didn't give me much of a choice in that regard."

The girls bounded up, hand in hand. Now that she had strength-enforcing support, Pyper pointed toward the hallway outside. "Come on, Mr. Tyler. We wanna show you now!"

He found himself led away from the activity center. It still amazed him. Amy. A mother. He tried to check for a wedding ring, but couldn't get a good look at the third finger of her left hand.

Pyper and Annie entered a brightly lit classroom where a petite, blonde-haired lady reassembled the space; she turned to greet them with a smile. "Hey, Pyp! Hey, Annie! What's going…" The woman's gaze rested on Tyler and she stopped short, her mouth hanging open. Her eyes went wide. "…on…?"

Tyler stifled a laugh. He was becoming used to fan recognition as his career progressed, but still, the reactions left him humbled.

Amy chuckled, and the sound tickled Tyler's ears. "Monica Edwards, meet Tyler Brock." Amy faced Monica again. "Pyper mentioned something about drawings the kids made while you conducted the nursery tonight. We wanted to catch a glimpse of their handiwork."

"Oh, yeah. Mm-hmm—" Monica didn't even blink. Instead she stared at Tyler, and the word *dazed* crossed his mind as a descriptive.

Annie stepped up, wielding a pair of pictures. "This is my house, and this is my church. See how I did the bell tower? Plus, mommy planted lots of pretty flowers for spring at our house. See?"

After Tyler checked them over and doled out appropriate praise, Pyper came to the fore and spoke, presenting her own creations. "This is church, too. It's like Annie's 'cause we go to church together and everything 'cause we're bestest friends. And this is mountains. I heard about them in school from Miss Monica. I *love* mountains."

Mountains. Tyler focused on that aspect of the drawing he studied and admired, realizing he might be able to use it to build a comfort zone for Amy's daughter. "Know what, Pyper? I live near mountains. You can see them from my house. Ever hear of the Smoky Mountains?"

Now that she was his sole focus, Pyper's shyness returned with a vengeance. She ducked her head. When she reclaimed her pictures, she kept her gaze on the floor while she fiddled with the papers. She scuffed the tip of her sandal against the tile at her feet.

Tyler focused on Monica Edwards, giving her a smile. She had regrouped following his arrival and struck him as the warm and engaging type. Besides, he wanted to give Pyper some breathing room. "You're a teacher?"

"I sure am. I own and operate the daycare center

where Annie and Pyper spend their days."

"And Sunny Horizons is also where I work during the winter and school months." Amy stepped forward, giving Monica's arm an affectionate squeeze. "She's a godsend."

What about spring and summer? Tyler wondered. *What do you do then?* He remained consumed by curiosity, and a desire to know everything possible about this new, matured version of Amy Maxwell.

Monica huffed out a teasing laugh. "Oh, you're just being biased. I'd take you full time, but winter and fall are the only points in the calendar year when I can pry you away from Jeremy. I'm going to finish cleaning this up. Tyler, it was great to meet you."

Jeremy? Calendar? Pry her away from what? Was Jeremy Amy's husband? Questions continued to spin in an assault of sorts. Nothing added up yet, but his heart begged for answers. "It's good to meet you, too. And thanks for handling the nursery tonight. What a huge help for the families."

"It was my pleasure…" She hesitated. "Although, it sure would be an excellent consolation prize if…"

Tyler heard Amy snicker, and once again, his heart flipped at the happy sound. In fact, he turned to her automatically, just in time to see her lift her camera and arch a brow. "Would you like a picture?" she asked Monica.

"You don't have to ask me twice!" In haste, Monica stepped up to Tyler's side amidst a round of laughter. She peered up at him apologetically. "I also brought my copy of your new CD. Do you think you'd mind… ah…"

He didn't need a compass. "I'd love to sign it for you." Charmed, Tyler set out to reassure. "It's the least

I can do after all your help tonight."

The photo-op was interrupted when a man entered the room, hand in hand with twin children, a boy and a girl, who appeared to be of Asian descent. "Hi, JB!" Amy's greeting was addressed to the adult, but then she bent to tweak the boy and girl on their noses. "Sam and Katie, how are you?"

"Ready for home, I think." JB laughed, and the sound was deep and rich—as though it was something he did often. He stepped up to Monica and gave her a kiss—then a rueful grin. "I think they're finished with church, Monica. They had a bit too much fun with some fruit juice that cost us a big stack of napkins."

Monica cringed, but she giggled, too. "They were angels in here during the concert. I asked Lisa to take them to you so I could clean up; I'm nearly finished." JB, who had a strong, tough build, easily hefted the children. Monica stepped close. "Were you guys good for Daddy while Mommy was away?"

In perfect unison, the kids turned wide, innocent eyes on their mother and nodded emphatically. Monica took their hands in hers and placed kisses on both chubby fists.

Amy gave a formal introduction to Monica's husband, Jeremy Edwards, and some of Tyler's panic dissipated. "I think we need to make this photo a family affair. Why don't we have Amy take a shot of all of us?" he offered.

Monica looked at him with adoration in her eyes. "Know what? You're even sweeter than I thought you'd be. Thanks!"

Monica's heartfelt gratitude warmed him. In a moment of praise, Tyler gave silent thanks to God for being able to live out such an enormous life blessing.

Then, in deference to the picture, his eyes focused on Amy.

૰ૐ

As he followed Amy back to the main assembly room, Tyler's cell phone vibrated in the front pocket of his jeans. Since Amy walked ahead with Pyper and Annie in tow, he slid it free and flipped it open. One missed call—and a text— from an increasingly familiar phone number. Since a text message would be quicker to deal with than a direct phone call, Tyler opted to open that rather than check his voicemail.

Hope the Woodland concert was all u hoped. We need 2 talk when ur back in TN. Urgent – 4 ur good – n I admit it – mine 2. KR

Tyler shook his head. Often, when assaulted by frustrations—and mounting anxiety—he had to battle back the desire to bite off a mild curse. This was just such a moment. He took an extra second to scroll through calls he had received during the past few weeks. A large chunk of the electronic demands came from the author of his latest text. This very powerful, deliberately persuasive person tempted Tyler with an offer most artists would beg to claim. Not Tyler, though. Instead, he fought temptation by simply refusing delivery.

But time was running out on that particular option.

"You all set?" With Pyper in her arms, Amy turned to face him, her brows drawn. Tyler snapped to attention, now realizing she had stopped at the threshold of the activity center. The facility had grown considerably quieter as people left Woodland. His fingertips moved restlessly against the phone while Amy puzzled over his delay.

He fixed a smile into place. "Absolutely. Sorry. Just a bit distracted by a piece of business I need to take care of once the tour is finished."

The explanation sufficed; in fact, the way Amy looked at him, he could read how impressed she was, and he wanted to sigh. He wanted to tell her that it wasn't as awe-inspiring as people thought. It was tough sometimes, holding on to faith and your principles, especially in the entertainment industry.

For now, though, he kept quiet and found relief in the fact that he had dodged another round of electronic prodding from a troubling suitor.

With Amy at his side, Tyler met up with his tour mates and began making the rounds to say goodnight. Dave Wells, his tour manager and closest friend, joined their circle. In typical fashion, Dave wasted no time on preamble. He jiggled his own cell phone from his fingertips. "Rossiter is on the hunt for you, Tyler. Again. And again...and again..." For dramatic effect Dave's voice trailed off and his lips twitched into a wry curve.

Tyler scowled. "Wait a sec. Now he's tracking me through *you*?"

Dave offered a good-natured shrug. "So it would seem."

"Sorry for that." Tyler firmed his lips, noticing the exchange held Amy's full attention. He gathered in a stilling breath, uncertain about having her witness the pressures he had to endure.

"Not a problem. Sometimes running interference is part of my job. But, you know, maybe if you just *talk* to him?"

"I will." Tyler knew he sounded harsh. "When I'm ready. Kellen Rossiter is pushing, and he knows it. I don't like being pushed. Not about my career." Tyler let a sharp, punctuating pause follow his declaration. "Maybe my silence will clue him in that he's being annoying."

Dave's brows lifted. He pursed his lips and slid his fingertips into the front pockets of his jeans. "It's also flattering. Don't kid yourself into thinking you're not impressed by his attention, Tyler." Delivering a final, pointed look, Dave rocked back on his heels then walked away.

Tyler closed his eyes and flexed his jaw.

Amy remained a silent, though increasingly curious, observer. At length, she gave him an encouraging look. "OK. That was interesting."

"Just a business fire to deal with; that's all."

"Oh? Can I ask what's going on? Who's this Rossiter person?"

In an instant, everything faded from his world but Amy. He saw them as they used to be back in high school, best of friends, sitting side-by-side on the well-worn couch of his parent's family room after school, sharing their latest problems—or dreams. Oh, how he missed that connection.

But now wasn't the time to dive deep.

Tyler stiffened his stance, wishing like crazy he could just pour out his heart to her

But this wasn't the place.

Exhaustion crept through his system, coloring his attitudes about everything, even Kellen Rossiter. *Especially* Kellen Rossiter. Post-performance adrenaline leaked out of him like sand particles, depleting his energy by the second. For now, it would be best to turn in for the night and try to come out fresh after some rest.

"It's a long story. Hey, will you be around tomorrow?" He didn't mean to sound quite so eager, but there was no way he could mask his feelings.

"I've been invited to Pastor Ken's for dinner. But I'm just not sure about going…I mean…"

She attempted to shrug the idea aside, but, tired or not, Tyler operated on high alert when it came to Amy; it was time to dispel her doubts as quickly as possible. "Please come. I really want to catch up with you."

He wouldn't beg; he kept his voice steady. Following the pattern of their past history, he simply laid out the call of his heart and then let her, and God, decide what was meant to be. Noble, sure; but on the inside, just like in high school, he quaked. Amy was his most vivid, stirring crush, the first love he'd never forgotten nor entirely released. To do so, he had discovered, was impossible. For as long as he was in Michigan, he wanted to spend as much time with her as possible.

"Are you sure?" Her words were so quietly spoken he nearly missed them. Now Tyler puzzled. He stared into her eyes, letting her see the questions he held there. "Why would you even need to ask me that? Of course I'm sure."

He stepped in close and glided his hand against her arm. He couldn't get over the changes in her, especially the diminished spirit and verve. Dinner plans were fine enough, but dinner would provide only a couple of hours together.

Earlier that evening, just before Tyler spotted Amy getting ready to leave, Pastor Ken had invited Tyler and his parents to a day of boating and swimming on

Lake Saint Clair. Ken and Kiara had recently purchased a pontoon boat. Since the day promised to be gorgeous, and overly warm, the idea of a relaxing cruise, free of outside distractions, became the agreed to itinerary for tomorrow afternoon.

Tyler kept quiet on that count for the time being. An idyllic plan swirled into place with a reviving power that pushed back a bit of his exhaustion. As seconds ticked by, his idea developed substance, and fast, strong roots. Before leaving Woodland and going home with his folks tonight, he'd float the idea of including Amy and Pyper. He imagined Ken would be happy to have them join the party.

Thoughts of professional pressures, and hard decisions to come once his tour concluded, vanished in the face of being with Amy again. They'd have a bit of uninterrupted, one-on-one time. They'd have an opportunity to swim, lay out in the sun, and talk. *Really* talk. Throw dinner into the mix and they'd end up with the full day together.

After that, reality would set in. But for now, if Ken agreed to the plan and Amy accepted, they'd have tomorrow.

4

The last thing Amy wanted to do was sleep.

It was close to midnight when she pushed gently and quietly through the door of her second-floor apartment; Pyper was sound asleep, a heavy but pleasant weight in Amy's arms. She moved as gingerly as possible, not wanting to disturb her daughter.

They had stayed too late at Woodland, but any excuse she could find to spend a few extra minutes with Tyler left her feeling like a fairytale princess doing battle against the fade of a magical spell. *Tyler.* Amy's lips curved. Something deep in the core of her body melted without resistance. The reaction couldn't be helped because it was so incredibly good to see him again.

She tiptoed toward Pyper's room, making her way through the darkened house by rote. Once there, she pulled back the blankets and laid her daughter on the bed. She unbuckled and prepared to remove Pyper's sandals. One shoe was off, and she was working on the second when Pyper tossed a bit, and gave a breathy, unintelligible sound.

Amy stopped just long enough to brush a hand against her daughter's satiny curls. She marveled at the serenity reflected on Pyper's face. A degree of love washed through her so powerfully it left Amy's chest to ache. For a moment, she simply adored her

43

slumbering child. She gave thanks once more that Pyper had become her miracle, born from the tragedy of her marriage. "I already love you to the depths of my soul, little girl. How is it possible I keep loving you more and more every day?"

Pyper rustled, but never fully roused, nor opened her eyes. "Mommy," she whispered contentedly.

With that, she snuggled in deep, and Amy finished bedtime preparations, certain Pyper was now lost to the world until sunrise ushered in a new day. "If only I could rest as easy."

She kissed Pyper's forehead then exited the room. In passing, she clicked on the living room lights. She was at loose ends. She had a lot to think about, but couldn't bring herself to focus on a single thing except the image of Tyler Brock. She looked around her simply furnished living room; there was a used but still lovely and comfortable sofa, a wooden rocker she'd found at a garage sale, end tables and mismatched but pretty brass lamps. She couldn't stay focused, or relaxed, and she knew precisely why.

She knew what she wanted to do, but...

"Bad idea," she chastised herself, perching her hands on her hips. "Memory Lane needs to shut down for a little while."

As usual, though, her heart overruled her head. She crossed through the open, spacious layout of her apartment to a storage closet located at the end of the hallway near the bedrooms. There, from the second shelf, she pulled down one of two photo albums. Every possession that pre-dated her marriage to Mark was gone now. Not that there had been much to begin with. Still, she was a memory box kind of girl. Always she had stashed away odds and ends from her life and its milestones; she had treasured them with a heart that was inherently sentimental. Now, everything was history, relegated to memory alone.

Except for this gift from Kiara.

She reached to the shelf above and grabbed a thick, cozy afghan her mom had given her a few months ago and then made her way back to the living room.

She curled up on the couch, tucking her feet beneath the warm blanket while she settled in. Slowly she opened the cover of the album. The first thing she came upon was the birthday card that had accompanied the gift. Amy flipped it open, already feeling the sting and build-up of tears. She could practically quote its inscription from memory:

Amy:

On this day especially, allow yourself to remember. Remember who you are, and who you long most to become. You're a remarkable lady destined for remarkable things.

"For I know the plans I have for you," declares the Lord. "Plans to prosper you and not to harm you; plans to give you hope, and a future." Jeremiah 29:11

I know you've missed having this memento—among many other things. I hope you enjoy it. It's a replication of all the photos you gave me and Ken after the mission trip to Appalachia. They're the work of your hands, the mission through your loving eyes. I hope it helps you recognize the fact that you possess such a beautiful servant's heart.

Love you, Miss Thing. Kiara

Amy bit her lips to stop their trembling; her throat

was tight, and she brushed her fingertips beneath her lashes. She turned the pages gently, smiling now as image after image worked through her spirit like a cascade.

Memories crested in, her tired mind just lax enough, and vulnerable enough, to let them have their way with her.

The shot of a group campfire was beautiful, full of oranges, reds, and yellows. Sparks floated toward the sky as Tyler led the group in a song on his beloved guitar. In the picture, she sat to his right; her old fried Carlie Jamison sat to his left, on a thick, downed log in front of the fire pit. This was one of the few pictures Amy was in, because David Parker had insisted on finally getting her in a shot.

"It's tough being the photographer," he had said. "You never seem to be part of the action. Go on. Get in there and join the group."

Amy smiled, stroking the plastic cover of the photo as she noted the way Tyler was lost to whatever song he played. She was leaning forward to watch him, a friendly smile on her face. Carlie, on the other hand, watched him in an open adoration that had gone unnoticed by Tyler.

Similar to Tyler, almost perfectly suited to him in fact, Carlie had no problem at all leaving her heart bare. Amy recalled the whispered conversation they had shared in their bunkhouse after that campfire.

"He's awesome, Amy. I don't know why you'd ever push him aside." The two of them had squeezed onto Amy's narrow cot. Beneath the blankets they hid a flashlight's illumination and whisper-chatted. Carlie harrumphed. "I wish he weren't so hooked on you. If he weren't, he'd realize you're not interested, and focus outside of that crush of his. I mean, like, the two of you aren't ever meant to go anywhere, right? Then, he just might discover someone else who could be just as good."

Amy couldn't disagree. "I hear you. I know what you mean. It's just…I can't help it, C. It's not that I don't like Tyler. In a way, I'm flattered by the way he always thinks of me, and sticks close. I'm not trying to string him along or anything, but he always treats me so good. I know he likes me. And I'd be stupid not to like him back—as a friend and all—but I just can't stop thinking about Mark Samuels! I swear, he wires me like no other! He's *so* incredible! I can't believe someone as popular and awesome as him is interested in me! Tyler's great and all, but Mark is…like…" With wide eyes and a waving gesture that ruffled their covers, Amy encompassed the very air, the very universe around them. The two of them burst into giggles.

"OK, then do me a favor."

Amy giggled again, and they squiggled for a bit of extra room; the beam from the flashlight slid erratically across the light-dousing blanket. "Anything for you, C."

"Will you let me sit by him on the way home?"

They burst into a fit of full-fledged laughter that stirred the restful breathing patterns of their bunkmates, chaperone Kiara Jordan included, but they toned it down promptly and cricket sound, leaf chatter and undisturbed night air, returned.

"That's a deal. Enjoy."

The echo of those words took the edge of a scalpel deep and sure to Amy's heart, causing her mind to scream: *God help me.* Her heart began a heavy thud.

How blithely she had given away solid gold while grasping instead for the seduction of sparkling, but meaningless, glitter dust.

Oh, Mark had been interested all right, just as Amy hoped. In fact, he had asked her to the homecoming dance less than a week after her return from Pennsylvania. For a time, Carlie and Tyler had ended up going together as well, once Tyler got the message loud and clear that Amy's heart was held firmly by the school's basketball team captain and most popular star. Their senior year went somewhat cold as a result, and as soon as graduation hit, their paths split into completely opposite directions.

Almost immediately, Tyler left Michigan, opting to spread his wings and stay with his aunt and uncle in Nashville. Before departing, he told his friends—Amy just barely included—that he was on his way to Tennessee to make a mark in the only arena that mattered to him from a professional standpoint. Music.

Amy had continued her heady, electric relationship with Mark. Passion in all its forms ruled her world, blinding her to the consequences of being reckless and emotionally intoxicated. They saw one another constantly, feeding off the irresistible pull of physical desire. Still, somehow, Amy had never believed an unplanned pregnancy would happen to her—the queen of the school—nor to Mark, its undisputed king. They made love, surrendering completely to the pull of their minds, and their bodies, repeatedly savoring every new connection they discovered.

Until the moment Amy found out she was carrying his child.

But even then, she clung to the absolute belief in

happy endings. Certainly, theirs was a critical error in judgment. Yet by God's grace alone, Amy held to Pyper's conception and birth as her life's greatest blessing.

She knew once they married, they would be happy. As a couple, and a family, they would make a way together. But it hadn't turned out that way. Amy's chin quivered as she continued to page through the photo album. How could she have *ever* been so naïve?

She flipped through a few more pages, and a wavering smile replaced tears as she studied a photograph of Kiara kneeling in the front yard of the home they had renovated, with two of its four occupants: twins Amber and Alyssa Kidwell.

Amy's gaze moved to the colorful beaded bracelet Kiara had on her wrist. Amber had made it for Kiara's and Alyssa had created an identical bracelet for Amy — a thank you to two of the people who, by virtue of elbow grease and donated time, made their mother's life a bit easier and more civilized. The two little girls had shown maturity far beyond their years when they recognized the change in their circumstances, and their mother's outlook that had been brought about by the help of the Woodland team.

Alyssa had lovingly placed the piece on Amy's wrist and Amy had refused to remove it for long months afterward. When she did take it off, she had tucked it safely away, never wanting to forget the love behind its creation.

Amy's gaze strayed to her empty right wrist, and she got choked up all over again. The bracelet was gone, left behind in her desperate escape from abuses both physical and mental. Amy blew out a breath, wishing she could will the bracelet, and the innocence of that missionary period, back into existence.

She sniffed back tears. This trip down memory lane was making her an emotional wreck, but what a sweet, loving memory the photo stirred, as well.

Amy had been just as much an emotional wreck after Alyssa gave her the bracelet. The gesture was so selfless, so poignant. Amy had found it necessary to break away from the home rebuilding crew for a few minutes so she could regroup.

She closed her eyes and tipped her head upward, remembering how perfect the cobalt sky had been on that day. Ever-moving tree branches towered high above. Studiously she kept her back to the house, not wanting anyone to see her tears, though she knew her shoulders trembled. From behind, the crackle and snap of dry groundcover signaled oncoming footsteps.

"Hey, Amy. I wanted to check on you."

Something within her went soft and perfectly still when she realized it was Tyler. Rich and low, his voice possessed the power to caress her soul. She'd closed her eyes, letting herself privately savor his arrival, and his obvious, caring concern.

"I can leave if you don't want to be disturbed, which I'm pretty sure is the case. I wanted to make sure you were OK. If I'm bugging you or anything, I'll go. Really, no harm, no foul."

He barely got the words out. In a blind move, unwilling and unable to consider anything else but the sanctuary he offered, Amy spun and tumbled into him. As though mysteriously prepared for just such a reaction, Tyler took her in smoothly and held on tight, rubbing her back as they swayed, and buried their faces against each other's shoulders. Despite the morning's work, he smelled of appealing, musky spice, and his warmth radiated through her, dispelling the chill of the battle she recognized two small girls had to face each day as impoverished children. The slow glide of his caress across her shoulders soothed Amy's ache of sadness.

So, she sank into the moment, and let it go on. She tucked into him in an alignment that felt a lot better than it ever should have.

"Thank you," she whispered at last. But she continued to rest against him, taking in his strength. "You know what, Tyler? You deserve…"

Oh, Lord, she thought in a panic, *where is this sentence coming from, and where will it lead us?* Amy didn't lift her head from its comfortable resting spot against Tyler's shoulder, but her eyes popped open, and went wide.

"Yeah?" He pulled back just far enough to study her face. He tracked his fingers through wisps of hair that had floated from her loose ponytail. He didn't seek her eyes, or look at her with eager hope, or a giddy sense of expectation. Instead, he focused on the path of his hand, which moved now to her shoulder, and stayed in a gentle hold.

"Oh, nothing." She stammered the words, staring at him, stunned by this unexpected wash of longing.

He looked down, obviously deflated by her response; but he didn't make an issue of her stumble. He didn't let any sense of awkwardness remain. Instead, he grinned. "I see. So, I deserve….*nothing*?"

The tightness in Amy's chest eased; tension and the fear of hurting someone so dear to her evaporated as Tyler delivered the tease and then looked her straight in the eyes. "You deserve a lot more than nothing," she said. "C'mon. You know that. You deserve everything good. That's what I was going to say."

They remained together, his arms snug around her waist, her hands resting on his shoulders. But briefly, Tyler's gaze focused on the stand of trees around them, then the twigs and leaf clutter on the ground. "Yeah. Maybe."

"Try *totally*." Even if she refused to become romantic about Tyler Brock, he was special, a treasured friend, and he needed to know that. "Besides, I found out something."

"What's that?"

"Remember the game we played on the drive down here from Michigan? You had to compare me to a box of crayons, and you said I was colorful, like a rainbow. I had to compare you to a rubber band and I said you were musical, like a rubber band when you pull it tight and pluck it."

Tyler chuckled lightly, and she could have sworn he blushed a little bit, too. "Yeah, so?"

Suddenly she was desperate; she needed to assure him of his place in her heart, even if it wasn't the place he wanted most to occupy. She stroked her fingertips along his smooth jaw, and let herself bask in the open, honest beauty of his hazel eyes, if only for a moment.

"*So* what I found out is this: you don't need to be pulled tight in order to make music, Tyler. You do it naturally. Literally. You're really just a great, great person. Thanks for always being there for me. I notice it, and it means a lot."

He watched her for a time. Then, Tyler inched closer—just a trace—almost as if he couldn't help himself. Amy lost her breath, caught between the fear of what might come next and the wish and the hope that he'd close that brief space of air between them and take her on a long, free-fall of a dizzying kiss.

Her lips went dry, but lax. Her entire body tingled. His head dipped just a bit lower, and Amy's hold on his shoulders tightened in expectation. The tingle morphed into a deep-seated ache. His eyes focused on hers, intense, mature in feeling and awareness far beyond that of a seventeen-year-old.

Tyler displayed such tenderness, and soul-deep emotion that she nearly stepped into the unfamiliar terrain of reevaluating and leaving behind everything her budding heart yearned for and wanted most to grasp.

In this moment, she caught a promise of all she somehow knew, deep inside, Tyler Brock would one day become. It was a glimpse so powerful it tempted her heart into uncharted territory, because all the signs of a potent, ordained emotion were right there in front of her.

She almost skimmed her hands upward against his neck, almost trailed her fingertips through the slightly dampened ends of his hair; she almost drew him down of her own accord. Somehow, she knew he'd taste wonderful. Somehow, she knew he would guard and treasure her heart.

In the end, though, *almost* carried no weight and the moment passed.

Following a lengthy silence, intensity diminished. Expelling a quiet sigh, Tyler froze. His tongue coursed his lips, which drew her fascination and focus. He continued to hold her, and they studied each other's eyes. He remained comfortably in place, his arms still a welcome, promising circle against her waist. Amy flushed shyly, lowering her gaze, unprepared for this influx of heady, magnetic feeling toward Tyler Brock of all people.

Like a fool, she had stepped back. Instead of casting aside her preconceived notions, she took possession of his hand in a casual, friendly manner, and they returned to the front yard of Casey Kidwell's home to resume their assigned landscaping detail.

Amy blinked hard, still able to recall the warm, somewhat work-roughened texture of his hand in hers. She re-found her focus, and the present moment, but not without the sharp ache of regret.

"You opted for arrogant, troubled, and controlling instead of gracious, loving, and tender-spirited." Her murmured chastisement cut the silence of the empty living room. In a resolute motion, she closed the album and set it aside. "Way to go, Maxwell."

Yep, this pretty much clinched it. There was no way she'd ever be able to sleep tonight.

She straightened abruptly as it occurred to her she needed to take care of uploading the concert pictures. That would give her something productive to do. After all, first thing in the morning, members of the standing-room-only audience would be clamoring for the concert and meet-and-greet photos. She padded to the entryway of her apartment, where she had dumped her purse and equipment bags in deference to putting Pyper to bed. She pulled out the camera and went to her bedroom, where she sat down at a small desk, before a glowing computer monitor.

She booted up, extracted a USB cord from the drawer and connected her camera to the terminal. During the next few hours, she downloaded and labeled photos, setting up a page at the Woodland Church website to commemorate Tyler's concert.

Joy welled up as she worked. Image after image clicked through her increasingly relaxed and sleepy mind, soaking into her thirst-driven heart with each moment she spent creating the concert page. She went a bit unsteady when one particularly striking photo filled her monitor. This one was a solo shot of Tyler, centered perfectly in the frame and backlit by multi-colored stage lights. Such a handsome man. The number of hits on the Woodland site was going to be astronomical tomorrow.

Tomorrow. What should she do about tomorrow? Giving a moan, too tired to properly consider what to do about Ken and Tyler's dinner invitation, Amy checked her email before shutting down her computer.

Five unanswered e-mails from the top was a note from Pastor Ken's address with a subject line that read: *Life's Too Short.*

Puzzled, Amy clicked it open.

Hey, Amy –

I think I can speak on behalf of everyone who attended Tyler's concert, and the meet-and-greet, in saying thanks for all your hard work tonight. I can't wait to see the pictures.

As a reward for your efforts, but mostly because we enjoy you both so much, please bring Pyper and join Kiara and me, and the Brock family, for a day of boating and relaxation on Lake Saint Clair. You've really earned it, and since life is too short to waste a single day of beautiful, late-spring weather in Michigan, I hope you say yes. After all, this is the least we can do.

Let me know as soon as you can. We're trying to plan a lunch menu for the boat trip, and don't forget about dinner afterwards. We'd meet up at our house at around 11 o'clock and take off from there.

God bless, and thanks again, Amy. You're a godsend ~

Ken

Amy stared at the missive; she clicked on the reply toggle because she knew she had to respond quickly. Then, she sat stymied, unable to construct anything. *The Brock family.* Tyler would be there. She wasn't committing to just dinner with him, but an entire day of boating fun. More opportunities to...what? Reconnect? And what about his duet partner? Sure, when they'd spoken after the concert, Tyler had acted as though Amy was the only woman in the world. But what about Rebecca? Amy drummed restless fingertips against the keyboard, waiting for words to form. Naturally, the idea of spending a gorgeous Saturday boating along the pristine waters of Lake Saint Clair held tremendous appeal. Pyper, of course, would go nuts at the prospect of spending a day with Annie. She couldn't say no, and frankly, she didn't want to.

But at the moment, her heart was a tangled mess.

Not allowing herself a chance to second-guess, Amy typed out an acceptance, thanking Ken for thinking of her and Pyper. She clicked send. There was no future in this interlude with Tyler, of course, but she wanted to see him again, and spend the day with him. Owning up to that realization helped her understand how miserable she'd feel if she denied herself this last bit of time with him. For old time's sake.

She rubbed at her increasingly heavy, gritty eyes. It was almost three o'clock in the morning. "It's already tomorrow," she murmured, extinguishing her desk light and turning off her monitor. She climbed into bed shortly thereafter, equally divided between excitement and melancholy.

The day ahead would have to fill her up for a long, lonely time to come.

5

Tyler rolled out of bed, thoroughly refreshed and energized. It felt so good to be home. Smells from the kitchen prompted a smile. Certain things were a weekend tradition, like the aroma of fresh brewed coffee, the added smell and sizzling sound of cooking bacon and sausage, dish clatter, and muffled conversations as his mom and dad prepared a batch of fluffy scrambled eggs. He closed his eyes and breathed it all in. Riding just beneath the surface of those scents was the subtle spice of onion and green pepper; there was probably cheese in the mix as well.

"*Mmm* is it good to be home," he murmured, pulling on a t-shirt and sweatpants so he could indulge in his morning necessity: a large, strong hit of coffee.

Yawning, he left his bedroom behind, following the siren call of delicious food. He worked his fingers through the waves of his hair as he entered the kitchen. Staying in his old room, at his parent's home in the Shores, filled him with déjà vu—but in the best sense of the word. He smiled at the vignette he came upon at the stove. Side by side, his mom and dad moved in synchronization, buttering toast, cooking eggs. His bare feet didn't make a sound on the tile. He sneaked up behind his mom and gave her a playful poke. "Morning."

She jumped, letting out a yelp of shock. She

whapped at his arm; his dad just laughed.

Tyler, grabbed a bistro-size mug from the nearby dish cabinet and filled it. He tipped his head back to check the digital clock on the stove. Nine o'clock. A prickle of anticipation went live inside him. Two hours. Just two short hours and perhaps he'd be seeing Amy again...

"We made bacon and sausage. They're keeping warm in the oven." His dad turned to offer a nod, and he arched a questioning brow, forcing Tyler away from his thoughts. Temporarily. "You in for a few of each?"

"You bet." He wondered if Amy had accepted the invitation Ken promised to send. Had she seen it yet? He looked at his mom, setting an arm around her shoulders for a second. It felt good to be back in the care of his folks for a couple of days. "Can I help you at all?"

"Nope. We're ready. Have a seat and we'll eat."

He ignored her request to sit and instead fell into his old habit of grabbing a pot holder so he could help pull dishes out of the oven and carry them to the table. The gesture, he noticed, left his mom to smile nostalgically, her eyes to grow a bit glittery. He delivered the food, then pecked her cheek when he passed, returning to the kitchenette with his cup of coffee now in hand. "I sure have missed you guys."

"I know the feeling," his mom said. "Now sit."

"Yes ma'am."

The meal was a glimpse of heaven, his favorite, plus he hadn't eaten in—Tyler tried to figure out the hours and failed. A long time, anyway. In ravenous quiet, he devoured breakfast, his energy and attention on the rise.

"I noticed you touched base with Amy Maxwell

last night." His mom offered a plate of still-warm toast, and Tyler helped himself. Her comment caused his focus to zoom in and stay put. "I'm so glad she's back at Woodland. She's always been so sweet, and her daughter is such a cutie-pie. We see them at church all the time now, but she was gone for a while."

Parents as informants. Tyler nearly grinned, but stifled the reaction. Why hadn't that thought occurred to him as an option to find out more about Amy?

"Back at Woodland?" Tyler spread a napkin across his lap and leaned forward. "Did she leave town or something? Where'd she go?" Waiting, he chewed on some toast.

His dad gave a light shrug. "Oh, she stayed local, but stopped coming to church after she got married. Kinda lost touch with the Woodland crew. Last thing I would have expected, since she was so active in the church and all." Tyler swallowed some coffee, waiting to hear more, wondering if his folks realized he was now riveted. "Who was it she married?"

"Mark Samuels," Tyler's mom answered. "You might remember him, Tyler. He graduated with you, right?"

Tyler nodded, but closed his eyes briefly, absorbing that piece of news. Not that it surprised him much. "Are they still married? She's going by the name Maxwell, after all."

His parents exchanged uncomfortable looks. "No," Mom replied. "They're divorced. He's in South Carolina now, I think. Isn't that what Amy told us a while back?"

"Yep." Tyler's dad finished up his meal by spreading a bit of strawberry jam on the remainder of his toast. "I don't know anything about what caused the divorce, though. All I know is that Amy used to be as effervescent as a fresh serving of soda pop. Now she's real quiet. Reserved, you know? Hesitant."

The exact same traits Tyler had noticed last night. "She sure wasn't that way back when I knew her. She put the confident in confidence."

His parents chuckled at the comment, but sadness layered the sound; Tyler understood the reaction, because Amy *had* changed. Life had walked in on her and delivered an obvious blow. He wanted to know more. She had always been a faithful, God-loving girl. She had always found joy in helping others, and building her faith by sharing her time, talents—and even her convictions—with those around her.

"She works the spring and summer seasons at a construction company here in town." His dad stretched back and rested his hands on his stomach. "Edwards Construction. She's the office manager over there. Her boss, Jeremy Edwards, is a good guy. I know him from Woodland. His brother, Collin was your English teacher senior year, wasn't he?"

Collin Edwards, Jeremy Edwards. Connections fell into place. "He sure was. A great one, too. I liked him a lot."

Tyler's mom nodded. "And I've always liked JB. He and his wife Monica really helped Amy out when she came back to Woodland. During off-peak times in construction, Amy works at the daycare center and school that Monica owns. It's where Pyper goes. Sunny Horizons, I think it's called."

Tyler took in every nugget of information, storing each morsel carefully.

In a fond tone of voice, his mother continued. "I remember when you and Amy would hang out together after school, or before and after youth group meetings." She sighed. "If only things were different. She sure could use a good man like you in her life. I think she's afraid to reach out again. I have the feeling she was hurt, badly, but no one wants to intrude, or open up an old wound. Know what I mean?"

Tyler added that perception to the growing list of items he wanted to explore about Amy. He leaned back in the whaler chair he occupied. Discreetly he looked to the left and checked the stove clock once more. Almost ten o'clock. Would eleven o'clock *ever* get here?

"Need any help packing for our day on the boat?" Tyler offered his services to his mom, wanting to lend assistance, but also eager to burn off any amount of excess time that he could.

"Sure. Can you bring up the cooler from the basement and clean it out? My offering for the outing is veggies and cheese, plus some chips. There's also some pop in the fridge that we'll bring along. There are ice blocks in the freezer we can use to keep it all cold if you want to fish them out for me."

"Done."

Tyler took his dishes to the sink and rinsed them off. For a few moments, he stood at the kitchen sink and finished off his coffee. Gazing out the window, he absorbed the details of a good-sized backyard dotted by a couple of sturdy old maples. This is where he had grown up, where he felt most like himself. It was, unquestionably, home. Five years in Nashville hadn't changed that truth.

He smiled. The sky was a perfect blue, uninterrupted by even the tiniest cloud; the temperatures inched upward by the second. It was going to be warm—almost hot—and humid.

He fulfilled his mom's requests—which took him to ten-twenty.

Issuing a sigh, Tyler decided to take a shower. It would feel good to clean up, even though he'd just be diving into the waters of Lake Saint Clair before too long. Besides, he freely admitted to himself, he wanted to look good for Amy—and showering would eat up some more of the clock.

In his bedroom, Tyler pulled out a pair of swim trunks, a polo shirt and some toiletries from his suitcase. Preoccupied with thoughts of Amy, he was on his way to the bathroom when his phone chirped to life. He picked it up without a second thought. "Hello?"

"Well, it took me almost a half hour, but I finally got through to the Woodland website. I think they've reached their bandwidth. The pictures are great. The concert looks like it was amazing."

Tyler's pulse went into overdrive, and he swallowed hard. He had completely forgotten to check caller ID—a testimony to just how relaxed and distracted he had become since returning home. "Hey, Kellen."

Kellen Rossiter's low, appealing chuckle crossed the airwaves. "Good morning, Tyler."

Tyler paid pleasantries no mind. "The concert was good. I'm headed out in a bit though. Want to spend some time with my family before I have to hit the road again. What's up?" Unimpressed. Succinct and to the point. His words and tone presented just the image Tyler wanted to portray, even if his hands shook a bit.

"Then I won't keep you, but I've been trying here, Tyler. As I think you know."

"Yeah. By any means necessary."

Again came a rich, smooth laugh. "Don't expect me to apologize for that. All I want is a meeting, once you're back in Nashville. Tour's over in two weeks. When that happens, let's sit down, and talk, and find out if there's any reason for this cat and mouse game of ours to continue."

Kellen was relentless, and savvy. The man knew Tyler's schedule and everything. Tyler was annoyed on one level but, as Dave had correctly observed last night, he was extremely flattered as well.

"OK. Talk to Jess. She'll set you up." Tyler referred to his personal assistant, Jessica Farbare.

"I know she will, and I would have done that already, but I don't want to waste my time. Or yours. Before I set anything up, I want to know the answer to one question."

"Which is?"

A muffled sigh crossed their connection. "Are you interested in hearing what I have to say? I'm not sure how hard I can, or should, keep pushing. You've been doing an outstanding job of avoiding me. Frankly, I'm not used to that."

Tyler breathed, considered, thought and thought...and thought.

Kellen made a point. He wasn't a man people in his position typically avoided, under any circumstance. For good reason. Tyler pushed back the fear—fear for his soul, his convictions, and the entire pathway of his professional life.

"Brock, to a degree I understand where your uncertainty is coming from." Kellen's words were even and un-accusing. "I just want you to hear me out. No one's putting a gun to your head. I simply want you to listen to what I have to say." Silence passed. "Bottom line. Are you interested in taking a meeting or not?"

Kellen was forthright, yet ready to cut and run at this point—not that Tyler blamed him. As suspected, avoidance had run its course. If he didn't meet with Kellen, he'd regret it. Admitting to that truth, however, reeked of compromise. Potentially *dangerous* compromise.

Nonetheless, he had to be honest—with Kellen, and with himself. From there, he would trust God to move His purpose, and His grace, through whatever decisions might need to follow. With flutters erupting through his body, Tyler answered the question. "I'm interested. In a *meeting*. I'll listen to what you have to say, that's all I promise right now. Set it up with Jess and I'll be there."

"Fair enough, and thanks. Rest assured, she's my very next call."

Tyler didn't doubt it. Kellen Rossiter was on a mission—but would that mission best serve Tyler, and his career? Only God could answer that question, and Tyler was counting on His intervention and grace to do what was right.

Disengaged from the call, Tyler expelled a shaky breath. Well. So much for a day of escapism. Now Tyler was wired. Adrenaline pulsed through his veins; so did the thrill of possibilities and everything that might happen as the result of his music. Kellen's comments about the Woodland website left him intrigued. Tyler glanced at his laptop, which was open and humming. His computer rested atop a dark wood desk that had stood sentinel beneath his bedroom window for years. Since he had time to spare, he logged on, intending to explore. He was anxious to review Amy's photographic handiwork.

It took him a while. Kellen wasn't kidding about slow log-in times and spotty access. Were that many people logging on to review the chronicle of his concert? Really?

His brows pulled together. Tyler clicked, waited, clicked, propped his elbows on the surface of the desk and waited some more. He rubbed his stubbled jaw as the hourglass spun and lingered. At last, he made his way onto the "Welcome Home Tyler Brock" page and smiled with genuine amazement at what he found. Amy had captured it all. Picture after picture spoke not just of a concert, but a faith-filled event, full of life, energy and a family of fans that had been in his corner since his victory on *Opry Bound*.

Lord, what a ride that televised talent search had proven to be. The appearance had marked the dawn of his career.

Never had he expected to find his way onto a countrified version of American Idol, but, he had quickly run out of options. Fresh out of high school he had hit the Nashville pavement hard, knocking on the doors of every record label, talent agency, and musical connection he could think of in order to establish his dream. Fading fast one particularly hot and humid afternoon, he wandered through the doorway of Notes of Spirit, Inc., a talent agency that drew him in by virtue of its name alone. The agent he spoke with that day had forsaken representation in the face of a lack of experience—the story of Tyler's life thus far—but he had been encouraging. Tyler left the agency with an application in hand to join thousands upon thousands of hopefuls auditioning for next season's edition of *Opry Bound*—a CMT series that searched for the next, best country music star.

Tyler had been nervous, but figured: Why not leave this opportunity—like everything else in his life—to the hand of God? After all, this kind of opportunity is exactly what he had prayed for upon leaving Michigan and moving in with his aunt, RuthAnne Newman. God opened up the pathway; Tyler simply trusted enough to follow the call.

He plowed through week after grueling, draining week as the field narrowed. Performances led to evaluations, then rounds of fan voting and the agony of watching other talented, multi-faceted performers, many of whom became dear friends—like Rebecca Graham—get voted off.

But Tyler's music, his message, had a twist that seemed to intrigue the judges and audience members alike. Rather than performing pure country, or a combination of pop/country rock, Tyler focused on the music that spoke to him the strongest. His performances centered on contemporary Christian music that rolled straight out of his heart into the famed rafters of the Grand Ole Opry Theater.

At the end of it all, he had emerged victorious.

On a professional level, his life rocketed forward after the show results. He found himself the featured artist on thousands of Christian radio stations across North America. He made high-priced, glossy videos; he toured, and his name recognition began pulling in audiences at bigger and bigger venues. Last year culminated in Dove Awards for songwriting, and record of the year for the anthem that fast became his trademark, the duet he performed with Rebecca: *Amazing Grace.*

It sent a shiver down his spine that the mood and lyrics of the song seemed to somehow reflect the life and times of the one he missed most since leaving Michigan, the one who, even now, completed a piece of his heart: Amy Maxwell.

Clicking through the pictures, Tyler sensed Amy's spirit behind each photograph. And he yearned— yearned to know her all over again, in the here and now.

6

"Mommy, there's Annie! There's Annie!" Pyper yanked hard on Amy's hand. They moved forward, leaving their car in the driveway of Ken and Kiara's home. In tandem, they walked toward the front porch. The door rested open. Annie's light brunette head popped in and out of view as she bounded through the entryway inside and peeked out the door window, watching after them, and waving emphatically.

All of a sudden, Annie was swooped up into the arms of Tyler Brock. He swung her high while she giggled and squealed. That was enough of an image to stop both Amy and Pyper in their tracks.

She glanced at Pyper. A half-scared, half-resentful expression clouded her daughter's features. Pyper's hold on Amy's hand tightened and she looked up, her brows pulled tight, her eyes stormy. "Mr. Tyler is comin'? I didn't know Mr. Tyler was comin.'"

"Pyper, he's a good friend to Pastor Ken, to Miss Kiara and me, too." Amy dropped a beach bag and a small cooler at their feet and then knelt so she could be eye-to-eye with her daughter. "It'll be OK."

Pyper's down-turned lips and doubting eyes broke Amy's heart.

"He's nice? You promise?"

"Very nice. I *do* promise. You remember that from last night, don't you? Plus, you'll be so busy having fun with Annie you won't even have to worry about him."

The furrow between Pyper's eyes didn't ease. She looked toward the doorway, where Tyler and Annie waited—a cheerful picture that contrasted starkly against Pyper's dubious mood. Pyper rolled her lips inward, pressing them tight between her teeth, not moving forward quite yet.

Episodes like this battered Amy's soul. On the outside, her daughter looked the quintessence of little girl innocence. She wore a pair of white terry cloth shorts over the lower half of her orange and yellow polka dot swimsuit. Upon purchase, Pyper exclaimed she loved the swimsuit because it included a thick, matching headband that presently held her bevy of hair in place. Sunglasses were perched atop her daughter's head because Amy had a pair, too, and wore them just the same way. Pyper appeared every inch the picture of girlish charm, until she had to go face-to-face with a grownup man she didn't know. When that happened, she faded like a flower without water.

"OK." Pyper steeled her shoulders and firmed her jaw. "I'sorry, Mommy. I'll go. C'mon."

Heaviness pervaded Amy's spirit. Pyper didn't say the words because she was reassured. Body language and the false bravery that illuminated Pyper's eyes left Amy to realize Pyper offered the assurance only to please her mother. That made the moment twice as sweet, but ten times as heartbreaking.

Before re-gathering their gear, Amy leaned in to kiss Pyper's cheek. "I love you, snug-a-bug."

Pyper's wide, uncertain gaze touched hers. "Me, too."

Amy led the way to the front door. Pyper kept a tight hold on Amy's hand until Annie pushed open the screen door and yanked Pyper inside.

"You're here! Finally, you're here! We waited and waited!" Annie bounced, chirping with glee. "Mommy, Daddy, let's go!"

"Good morning, ladies. How are you doing?" Tyler's warm greeting encompassed Amy, but seemed to be directed mostly toward Pyper. Annie's presence certainly helped. In the company of her friend, Pyper assumed her more typical, sweet personality. She ran after Annie with gusto, but bypassed Tyler with nothing more than a short glance and a barely audible hello.

Amy's gaze met Tyler's, and she gave him a reassuring smile as she stepped inside and set her supplies on the ground. Once she straightened, she found herself wrapped in a hug from Tyler.

He was warm; his heartbeat next to hers was sure and steady. Hugging came as naturally to Tyler as breathing—she recalled that now. She used to be the same way, until life pulled a shutter over her emotions. The connection, while wonderful, also set her nerve endings on edge with an awakening sizzle.

"I'm so glad you came." His breath skimmed against the skin of her neck. He pulled back and took custody of her bags then gave Amy a directing nod toward the kitchen where, she assumed, food packing took place.

"I want gummi bears." Annie knelt on a nearby chair so she could oversee proceedings and help supervise her parents' efforts.

"Me too!" Pyper danced from foot to foot, peeking around Ken and Kiara, who stood at the counter, stashing foodstuffs. "An' don't forget cheese curls! I *love* the cheese curls!"

"Gotcha covered, kiddo," Ken gave Pyper a wink and Annie's hair a brief tousle when she left her chair and made a dash to stand by her friend.

In the meantime, Tyler gave Amy a look of mock offense at Pyper's food choices. Amy stared right back and shrugged. "She inherited my junk food gene. You're surprised about that?"

Tyler's easy laugh filled the room, causing Ken and Kiara to turn and greet Amy's arrival with a round of hugs.

But Amy's focus was all on Tyler. Dressed in loose swim trunks and a polo shirt of light blue, he moved through the kitchen, hefting a couple of grocery sacks and a cooler Kiara pointed to at the corner of the kitchen.

Ken clapped his hands together, eyeing the little girls like a conspirator. "Let's say we pack up the car and get outta here! Ready to hit the water?"

The enthused squeals of two delighted five-year-old girls was his answer.

∂∾⊸

"Here's a good spot. Let's drop anchor." Ken steered the boat slowly toward the shoreline—close, but far enough out that it felt to Amy as if they had a spot in the lake all to themselves. "According to the depth gauge, it's just over five feet. Should be perfect for swimming."

The engine came to rest and the boat began to float in a peaceful wake as the guys anchored the pontoon into place. Pyper and Annie, both safely secured in their float vests, sat next to Kiara and Mrs. Brock. The little girls started to squirm in their seats, chattering happily, as seagulls spun and cawed up above. A push of humid air crossed through the open space of the boat. Pyper and Annie shucked their shorts and shoes, which became a colorful heap on one of the padded benches. Amy and Tyler followed their lead, making ready to dive into the lake.

Amy joined the guys at the rear of the boat; Ken passed by, giving her a smile and a friendly squeeze on the arm when he made his way back to the pilot's chair. Ken was followed by Tyler's dad, who made passing remarks about a spiffy-looking powerboat that zoomed past. She sat down on the almost water level metal bench, hanging on to the nearby access ladder, and then made the critical error of dipping her foot into the water.

She promptly pulled free, shocked laughter bubbling up from her chest. "Cold! Ice cold! I am *not* swimming! *No* way!"

"*Way.*" Tyler sidled through the narrow space behind her and sat down. "If I'm goin' in, you're goin' in." He gave her a goading look. "And I'm definitely goin' in." They were side by side, shoulder to shoulder. Amy stole a glance his way and found him already tilted toward her, his eyes focused on her face, his lips turned upward just slightly. "Count of three. Then we jump."

Amy's eyes went wide with horror. "You're insane!"

"One."

"Tyler! No!"

"Two."

Her nerve endings sparkled, alive and

anticipating. Amy found her fingers suddenly and firmly entwined with his. "It's way too cold!"

"Three!"

Next thing she knew, she was pulled into the water as Tyler dove in. A mighty splash bubbled through the water. Cold surrounded her, but quickly went to temperate against her skin as she absorbed the shock.

A strong, warm arm slid around her waist, lifted her up then drew her in. Sputtering, shaking her hair back, Amy dragged her arm along the surface of the water, blanketing Tyler with a drenching arc. "You rat!"

But he wasn't finished yet. His hold tightened and before she could even scream, he lifted her up like a catapult, launching Amy through the water and above its surface before she crashed into the water once more, feeling like she had taken a brief, explosive ride through paradise.

But she refused Tyler the leverage of knowing how much she enjoyed his antics. Laughing on the inside, she emerged from the water and gave him a fierce glare. Tyler laughed at her and arched a brow in temptation. "Wanna go again?"

She found no way to refuse the smile that burst across her features. Moving through the water, she swam toward him. "Oh, yeah!"

For a few abandoned moments, they romped like kids. Sunlight sprinkled diamond dust along the rippling surface of the lake. The air around them warmed just as perfectly as the water cooled. Before long, Amy noticed Pyper approach the back of the pontoon. Pyper watched after them and Amy gave Tyler a quick look before swimming toward her daughter.

"Hey, Pyp." At the boat's access ladder, Amy dipped her head beneath the surface and quickly slicked back her hair.

After Kiara stepped up briefly to release the door lock, Pyper scrabbled to a sitting position on the rear deck, swinging her legs and stretching them downward until her pink-painted toenails brushed against the surface of the water. She kept her balance by holding on to the ladder rail while she studied Amy and Tyler. "That looks like fun."

Amy giggled. "It is. You want to come in and swim with us?"

Pyper regardedTyler for a long, intent moment. Slowly she nodded. "Mmm-hmm. Annie's gonna come in, too, though. With her mommy and daddy. But not for a few minutes."

The response was extremely tentative, but it was a "yes." Amy hoped to build on that; she wanted to make this confection of a day a joy for her daughter. The water surged and rippled next to Amy as Tyler approached.

He floated next to Amy, but smiled at Pyper. "Come on in and I'll give you a toss too, if you want, and if your mama says it's OK."

Pyper looked down, and then back up again. "It'd be OK. I got my vest on an' everything."

"It's cold when you first get in. After that, it's fantastic!" Amy backed away just far enough from the boat to give Pyper some room to jump. Then she held her arms open wide, waiting.

Pyper squiggled to a stand. She crouched, scrunching up her face as she launched forward. The splash drenched Amy, and left glittering drops to pour down Tyler's neck, shoulders and chest. Amy couldn't look away. Despite the chilly water, her body went warm; longing grew into a desire that sparked and sizzled against her senses.

When Pyper bobbed back up into Amy's arms, she squealed with shock and glee. "It's cold, it's cold, it's cold!"

"Wanna get out?" Tyler asked with a laugh.

"Nuh-uh!" Pyper started to paddle, suspended in place by her life jacket. She kicked, and sprayed even more water. She laughed. "I'm not even cold anymore. Wait 'til Annie jumps in. She'll be so scared! But I did it! She will too. I'll make sure. I'll make sure she knows it's OK." She kept paddling and kicking. "I wanna fly. Throw me, Mommy, throw me! Like Mr. Tyler did with you!"

Amy took a deep breath, and sent up a fast prayer. "You know, Tyler does throws a lot better than me. He's stronger."

"OK." Pyper's hesitance took the back seat—for a second, anyway. She turned back, looking at Tyler with wide, questioning eyes. "You won't scare me real bad, right?"

"Nope. I won't."

Her lips rolled inward. She nipped at them. Amy recognized how hard Pyper struggled to reach out in trust toward a man. *Help her, Lord. Please. Not every man is like Mark. Please. Help her to see that…*

"You *really* sure?"

Tyler's eyes went intent as he swam in, and took hold of Pyper at the waist, just below the chunky line of her day-glow float vest. "Sugar beet, I guarantee you this: I'll sink to the bottom before I let anything bad happen t'ya. Deal?"

Amy's lips trembled. Tears sprang to life, blurring the sight of Pyper relaxing completely and giving Tyler an expectant nod, a tenuous smile. Then, up she flew. A mighty splash blanketed them with water. Tyler swam toward Pyper. When she broke the surface, she howled with laughter. She scrubbed a hand over her dripping face and rubbed her nose. Then, Pyper speared Tyler with a teasing look. "That's silly, you know."

"What?" Tyler asked.

"Sayin' you'll sink to the bottom of the lake." Her features split into a wide smile, and her giggles danced across the air, carrying straight through to Amy's heart. "That's just *silly*, Mr. Tyler!" She doggie paddled and kicked across the distance between them. Not shy at all now, she grabbed on to Tyler's shoulders. "Again!"

Annie evidently had caught wind of the action in the water, and would not be denied her share of the fun. She fussed urgently with the rail latch of the pontoon. "Mommy, Mommy, my vest is on and everything! I wanna jump in! Le' me get throwed, too!"

Kiara barely made it to the back end of the pontoon before Annie freed the latch and made fast tracks to the boat's edge. She didn't look left or right. She didn't even flinch. Instead, she dived straight in.

Kiara chuckled, starting to remove her t-shirt and shorts. "I'll be right there! You may need some reinforcement."

Tyler's eyes tagged Amy's in a form of panic. "Kiara's not kiddin'. What have I unleashed?"

Amy didn't respond to the playful rejoinder. She was too choked up. He must have caught sight of the look on her face, the residue of her reaction to his interplay with Pyper. Tyler's puzzled gaze touched on hers, but then Annie paddled close, and the moment passed. Amy watched while he threw the girls and splashed through the water with them.

Kiara slipped into the water, issuing a brief exclamation of ice-water shock. Then, a pair of bright orange noodle-shaped floats splashed into place right next to Tyler and Amy. In unison they looked back toward the boat where Ken stood, watching them with somewhat of a knowing smile. "I thought those might come in handy if you want to just float, and catch your breath for a bit. Imagine the news flash if I allowed Christian music's hottest rising star to drown."

Tyler just groaned at that, but Amy's heart went full. Ken was right. Tyler had accomplished so much, and still seemed to remain true to himself. She was incredibly proud of him. They horsed around with the girls for a while longer, and then floated about in a boisterous game of Marco Polo.

Tyler swam up behind Amy and circled. He moved in close and looked into her eyes. Water, like silk, slid against her skin in a supple caress. Beneath the surface, their legs bumped from time to time as they dog-paddled, lost to one another.

"Guys," Kiara said over her shoulder, swimming for the access ladder, "I'm headed back to the boat to get lunch going."

"Wanna take a break?" Tyler asked Amy. "We could lay out and soak in some sun."

Amy nodded; after last night's marathon session and today's activities, she was pleasantly extended, both physically and emotionally. Her gaze tracked to the two fish-like five year olds who romped nearby. "You may have some trouble convincing Nemo-I and

Nemo-II over there to leave the water behind."

"Yeah? Watch me." Following a sassy wink, he faced the girls. "What's that, Amy? Kiara busted into the cheese curls and gummi bears? I say we better grab some before they're all gone."

Amy grinned, enjoying the way the two girls began a furious paddle to the boat. She gave Tyler a firm nod of respect. "Oh, man. You are *good*."

The girls climbed out first, with guiding support from Amy and Tyler. Tyler followed, but once Amy started up the ladder, he reached down, offering his hand to assist. She paused for an instant, already knowing his touch, the secure feel of his fingertips locked around her hand, would stir an electric echo through her insides. Looking at him now, she could barely recall his shy demeanor, his quiet ways. Those traits had evaporated; confidence and charisma now claimed their place. Some things, however, remind solid—his openheartedness, his faith, and a penetrating honesty in the way he engaged people.

Giving herself an internal shake, she accepted the gesture and absorbed the warmth that spread through her body. She stepped onto the rear of the pontoon and thanked him quietly. After they toweled off, Amy moved to join the others who occupied benches along the sides of the boat. She shook out her towel and prepared to lay it on an open space of the boat's floor.

Tyler took her by surprise when he claimed her towel and draped it over his shoulder. He had a smooth, supple chest. His shoulders and arms were well muscled and traced by lines of sinew that flexed as he moved.

Amy realized she ached; her longing built from the chest on out, radiating a slow, steady pulse of need.

"Let's go over here; it's a little quieter."

More private, remained unspoken. He retraced their steps to the rear of the boat. Everyone else began exploring food offerings, and Ken turned on the radio. Melodic, contemporary Christian selections filled the air. For Amy, everything faded to indistinguishable background noise. Her entire being zeroed in on Tyler Brock and stayed put. He laid out their beach towels. He stretched out promptly and sighed with delight. That was more than enough of an incentive for her to do the same.

Warmth seeped through the cotton towel from the metal flooring below, soothing her water-chilled body. She heaved a happy sigh, too. Ken had retracted the overhead canopy, so a clear sky, dotted by the spin and dip of birds stretched to the horizon. In a drowse, she closed her eyes.

"Delicious," Amy murmured unintentionally.

Tyler chuckled, the sound low and rumbling. She smiled in response, simply because it was such an appealing reaction to her verdict. They rested on their backs, side-by-side.

"Absolutely."

Waves lapped against the sides of the pontoon, a gentle punctuation mark of noise. The sound of nearby boats and muffled conversations, music and commercials, surrounded them for a moment.

"Can I make an observation?" Tyler asked.

"Sure."

"Well…" Their hands rested just a hairsbreadth apart. Tyler closed that distance and Amy nearly started when his fingertips slid softly, lightly against hers. Her eyes remained closed, but her body tingled. "You've always been beautiful. No question. But this.

Who you are now? You've grown into a truly breathtaking woman, Amy. And you've raised a spectacular little girl."

His subtle caress came to an end, but his touch continued when he covered her hand with his and let the connection linger. For the second time in less than a half hour, Amy was overwhelmed, instantly overcome by being treated so lovingly.

"Thanks." She spoke against a tight throat.

"So beyond that, here's what else I know."

Amy smiled to herself, drifting, relaxing. That new, subtle flavor of the south that now laced his words did something molten and liquid to her insides. "I know you work for a construction company and a school."

"Yep." She cleared her throat, deflecting her reactions as best she could. "I wish you could get to know JB. You two would really hit it off. He's a gem. And his wife, Monica, who you also met last night, is the one who owns the school where I work. She has a state-certified kindergarten program at her daycare center, Sunny Horizons. Annie and Pyper both go there."

"Sounds like an ideal setup."

Amy nodded, absorbing once more the absolute beauty of God's grace. "I couldn't possibly be more grateful. When I—" *Crashed,* she wanted to say, *when I made a fallen daughter's return to Woodland, JB, Monica, Ken and Kiara stepped forward with support that was both emotional and intrinsic.* Tyler, she realized at a quick, hand-shaded glance to her left, waited for more. "When I needed work, Ken gave me a referral to Jeremy's company. It was the start of summer, and Edwards Construction had a lot of work to handle.

Plus, his office manager resigned when she had a baby. Thing is, the job was only full-time work for half the year."

Tyler nodded, turning toward her now, leaning on his elbow so he could look down at her—and block the sun from her eyes. Amy unshielded her eyes and blinked, realizing the openness she longed to give him, the trust.

Much like Pyper, in a way.

"That's when Monica stepped in and offered me an assistant position at her daycare center. I work with the toddlers during the school year, fall to early spring. So it works out great. I get to be with Pyper more often that way."

Tyler's smile grew. "I think that's completely awesome."

Amy laughed, easing up the internal tension levels a bit. "Yeah. Me too."

Ken had tuned the radio to WMUZ, the Christian station in Detroit. A Britt Nicole song, Hanging On, drifted through the air. "And what else I know—" his voice was a slow and gentle leading. Amy knew at once this conversation was headed places. Big places. "—is that you ended up marrying Mark Samuels."

She had no excuse to hide her eyes. Tyler's position next to her blocked the blinding orb of the sun. Still, she reached for her sunglasses, and cleared her throat again as she did so. Tyler took hold of her wrist to still the motion before she could follow through. In emphasis, he slipped his thumb against her skittering pulse point in a light, but deliberate stroke.

"Don't put up a guard, Amy. Relax." The stroke continued, lulling. Assuring somehow. "Just talk to me."

She watched him, Tyler Brock, shadowed and framed against a pure blue sky. She refused to go tense and bitter with memory; she refused her past that kind of subtle victory.

And so, she confessed to the worst of it. "I divorced him, too. Best to get that out in the open, I suppose."

"My folks told me as much. I'm so sorry, Amy. I don't care how many years have passed, I know who you are, and I know for certain that kind of decision did *not* come easily to you. What happened, honey?"

The earnest question, the naturally delivered endearment, coasted into her blood stream and stirred up an emotional flood. Instantly she was carried away, her heart delivered to a place where she could reveal herself, and not fear for the consequences.

Patient and steady, he waited, watching her. She lay prone, oddly relaxed in contradiction to the increased tempo of her blood. She needed to see how close Pyper might be, and determine if she was within hearing distance. Amy lifted just far enough to see that her daughter was happily occupied by the companionship of the Brocks, who were presently being charmed out of a sandwich and some grapes.

Assured, Amy laid back down, tilting her gaze toward Tyler. "He…" Amy took in a breath. Like ripping off a sticky bandage, she came clean all at once, in a quiet, defeated voice. "He abused me, Tyler. Physically and mentally. And he took out a lot of his anger on Pyper, too. He'd startle her with unexpected, unwarranted spankings, he'd scream at her to be quiet whenever she cried, and he'd yell at the both of us for no good reason. Everything he did just seemed to scare her all the more. He couldn't hold a job, so his frustration grew by the day—and so did his use of alcohol as a way of escaping it all. When he started hitting me, I left." She shook her head. "And when I say I left, I mean there's absolutely nothing left of my old life. He saw to that quickly and efficiently."

She was so carried away by the admission, so wrapped up in the pain of a past she fought to move past every day of her life, she didn't realize until then that Tyler regarded her with steel-like eyes and a clenched jaw. Automatically Amy reached up, wanting to apologize for upsetting him. She stroked his chin and shook her head, whispering, "Hey…hey…I'm sorry…"

Tyler flinched. "Stop." He closed his eyes, taking deep breaths. "You mean to say he physically hurt you? Physically harmed you and Pyper?"

All Amy could summon was silence, and a nod.

"Gimme a sec."

Tyler seemed to lose his battle with control. He growled out a sound and sat up abruptly. A startling beam of sunlight crossed against Amy's face. She shaded her eyes. Tense seconds swirled past, so she reached for her sunglasses and slid them on. Moving into a sitting position, she slowly drew up her legs then encircled them with her arms. She rested her chin on her knees, watching him. Waiting, protectively sinking in upon herself.

"I can't even find it within myself to pray for him right now," Tyler whispered tightly, looking out across the water. In the face of his desolate, troubled admission, Amy ignored a round of laughter that came from their cruise mates, the song switched from Britt Nicole to a Point of Grace classic.

"No. Not right now. But you will. It took me a

while, too." When tense silence lengthened, she began to worry. "Tyler, talk to me. Please? What are you thinking?"

"That Mark Samuels doesn't deserve one precious second of the time God gave him with you, and that wonderful little girl."

Typical Tyler Brock. He was never, ever afraid to speak his heart. That was the beauty of him. Just like the words and melodies of his music, he laid it all out there and withheld nothing. Oh, how she admired that bravery of spirit.

Once, she had been the same way, but she had never been smart when it came to matters of the heart. Instead, she had opted to keep Tyler playfully enamored, a friend but nothing more while she chased after the bigger, better deal. Well, woe unto her. "I paid the price for being star-struck by the popular guy, the guy everyone admired. In theory, he was Mr. Right. In practice he turned into Mr. Devastation." She pursed her lips, and looked at her daughter. "And you've seen how hard it is on Pyper when it comes to adult men. It leaves me sick at myself sometimes."

Tyler leaned in and captured her chin gently in his hand. He looked intently into her eyes. "Don't ever, *ever* take responsibility for a man abusing you and your daughter, Amy. You've pulled sunshine out of the rain. Do you understand that?"

The words were kindly spoken, tender in a way, but she heard the reinforcing steel that went along with them. The force of his conviction unsealed a chamber of her heart where fear and loneliness had been caged for far too long. Set free at last, their power diminished as they performed a fast and final dance through her soul.

Through it all, though, Amy wondered where she could, where she *should* she go now.

7

The party moved to Ken and Kiara's lovingly maintained ranch-style house, and continued into the early evening, when everyone gathered around the dining table and shared memories, laughter, and a wonderful, grilled surf-and-turf meal of steak and shrimp kabobs. After dinner, Tyler wandered through the house during meal clean up and found himself in the family room. He trailed his fingers against the entertainment unit. Currently the stereo played quietly. Music was as much a fixture within the Lucerne's home as it had been on the boat that afternoon.

A song change on the radio left him rearing back, and blinking hard. "Hey, Ken?" he called toward the kitchen, "is that WMUZ you're listening to?"

"Nope. Should be WNIC. They play some great jazzy after-hours music."

Puzzled, Tyler moved slowly to the kitchen, feeling dazed. "You sure?"

Ken entered from the kitchen, nodding but looking confused by Tyler's questions. "I think so. Feel free to check it. Why?"

WMUZ was Detroit's Christian music station. WNIC played mostly adult contemporary selections, a few oldies, and a variety of soft rock. Tyler opened the cabinet door and checked the radio dial. Sure enough, it was WNIC. "'Cause they're playin'my song. Right now. They're playin' *Amazing Grace*. C'mere and listen!"

Ken's eyes went wide as he tuned in and made the connection. Meanwhile, Tyler watched Kiara spin away from the sink, where she stood with Amy, cleaning dishes. Ken's wife did a quick boogie dance and joined Amy in an excited shout. His parents, he noticed, rose from the kitchenette. As one, everyone charged for the family room..

Like the fans they were, his family and friends started cheering, and they all danced like adorable fools. That's when a word, and a feeling, crested over Tyler with the impact of a tidal wave. *Crossover*.

In more ways than one, is that what was going on here? Would a crossover circle around not just his music, but his life as well? Was he poised at the precipice of soul-deep compromise? Desperation clutched at Tyler's chest. He did *not* want to compromise.

But the plan, and the momentum, just might be out of his control—happening to him whether he wanted it to or not, whether he was prepared for it or not. His stomach clenched and shivers worked through him from head to toe.

"Is this from when you concerted at church, Mr. Tyler?" Pyper asked the question as she sashayed with Annie and the song continued.

"No, sugar beet, this is a recording I did in a studio."

"It's cool!" Annie exclaimed.

"It's the *best*!" Kiara rushed forward to give him a tight hug. "Tyler, 'NIC! Can you imagine? This is fantastic!"

"It's just as great when it plays on 'MUZ," he answered. Still, his hands trembled. Still, his heart reacted with a thundering, excited beat.

At the end of the song, the DJ came on. "That was *Amazing Grace*, performed by Detroit's own Tyler Brock who's home this weekend for a benefit concert at Woodland Church in Saint Clair Shores. We can see now why this young man is taking Christian music by storm. Congratulations, Tyler, and welcome home."

The DJ's send-off inspired a second round of enthusiastic chatter in the Lucerne home. Once his fan club retreated to the kitchen, he caught Amy's eye and tilted his head toward the doorway of the family room that led outside. He looked at her expectantly, and she nodded, picking up on the cue. The girls had run off to play in Annie's room; the Lucernes and his parents chatted companionably in the kitchen.

Amy mouthed, "Let's go."

Sliding glass doors led to the back yard and a spacious patio. Thanks to Kiara's talents, the back yard of the Lucerne's home was a haven of tranquility, a showpiece of her landscaping skills and a sharp eye for all things beautiful. A series of ground lights illuminated a cobbled pathway that curved along the perimeter of the yard. Just now, the lengthening shadows of early evening painted their surroundings.

The peace and quiet enveloped his troubled mind. It helped that Amy reached for his hand and held it while they began to walk. He wondered if she realized the gesture had come to her automatically.

"If hearing *Amazing Grace* that way doesn't give you an adrenaline rush, I don't know *what* will."

"Aw, it's not as big a thing as you might think." Tyler bent and plucked a pair of pale pink hyacinth from the bevy of colorful blooms that ran alongside the bricks. "I'm in Detroit. That's all. Someone at 'NIC found out about Woodland and decided to play the song is all. Not a huge deal."

A soft, cooling breeze skirted past. The early night air sang with cricket noise. He handed the flowers to Amy and she smiled, lifting them to her nose. Her hair, now loose from the ponytail she had worn all day, fluttered across her face as she breathed deep. Tyler watched her in fascination. He didn't need to be close to smell the sweet, rich aroma. A blanket of hyacinth framed in slightly taller snapdragons then well-shaped evergreen shrubs. Lilac trees dotted the fence line, and periodically the combination of scents carried through the yard, intoxicating and bursting with spring's renewal.

Despite the blows of life, Amy remained stunningly beautiful. Sure, she had gone for comfort and ease for their day on the water—wearing a simple shorts and t-shirt combo. The lavender colored one-piece swimsuit she had worn was discreet and basic as well, but none of that mattered. Even in flip flops and ultra-casual attire, she left him breathless.

Being near her, all he could think of was new life. New opportunity. The parallels caused Tyler to re-center as they continued their stroll. Between the airplay on WNIC, and Kellen Rossiter's heated pursuit, he was a lot more nervous about the way things were going than he wanted to let on. He needed to pull back a bit; he needed to think things through. Most of all, he needed to pray.

Amy interrupted his introspection. "Mainstream airplay is a huge deal, Tyler, and you deserve it." He was grateful for her loyalty, and pride, but she didn't understand the constant battle he fought to remain true to his principles when the call of celebrity, with all of its advantages, and all of its pitfalls, grew by the day. She twirled the flower stems gently. "You should tell Rebecca. I'm sure she'll be thrilled to hear the news."

That comment thoroughly diverted him from his anxieties. Tyler used his hold on her hand to turn her toward him. "Is there something you'd like to ask me about her, Amy?" When she didn't answer, when instead she watched him with wide, searching eyes, he reached up to brush his knuckles against her cheek. Sure enough, they were warm as toast. That made him smile, and gave him the courage to push a little. "C'mon. Ask me."

She shrugged in a negligent way, but her eyes betrayed her. Big time. That's probably why she looked away. "I think she's amazing. And she's very gifted. You two seem to get along really well."

Affection for Rebecca rose to the surface of Tyler's feelings, but that affection paled in comparison to what he held in his heart for Amy. Nothing had ever come close, and he somehow knew nothing else ever would. "Yes. We sure do. Now, Amy...*ask me.*"

She sighed, her brows furrowed. "Whatever the answer is, it wouldn't make a difference." He swore he heard tinges of regret woven through those whispered words. "I mean, you and I, we...we're friends, we're *great* friends, but...it's not like I have a hold...or like you owe me anything..."

The blurred edges of a relationship with this revised, grown-up version of Amy Maxwell gained new resolution. Her display of hesitant interest, an interest she couldn't seem to fight or deny, made his heart take flight. He slid his thumb lightly against the back of her hand. "You're stammering. Please, just ask me what you want to know."

Her soft sigh cut the stillness of the night that drew in around them like a blanket. "Is she…are you two…involved? Are you together in a romantic way?"

"No, honey. Not at all. If I were, I wouldn't have been on a boat with you all day, hanging on every last second we have together."

He watched her downplay the smile, stifle the sparkle that lit her eyes, but they were there, and they sang to him as perfectly as a well-crafted melody. Tyler leaned down. Before kissing Amy's cheek, he let his lips brushed against her jaw line, whisper against her neck. She smelled of an alluring spice, and vanilla.

"You two were on *Opry Bound* together." Her voice faltered, but she was obviously going for some semblance of control here. "You were competitors. That had to be hard."

He ignored her unsteady breathing pattern, and they resumed their meandering walk. "Yes, we were, but we were always friends, too. We connected from the start. It honestly broke me up when she got voted off. She was then, and is now, one of the few people who will ever understand how crazy and wonderful and difficult that whole period was. She's one of my closest friends as the result. But that's as far as it goes. For either one of us."

Something he'd said left Amy grinning like the young girl he remembered from high school, leaving him to puzzle as they nearly completed a circuit of Ken and Kiara's backyard.

"I have a confession to make," she said.

"Oh, yeah? It's good for the soul, you know."

"Ha, ha."

"What's the confession? I'm intrigued."

She shot him a bashful look. "Well. I dialed my fingers off voting for you when you were on *Opry Bound*."

"Really? You did?"

"Of course. I couldn't get over it. The sensation you created is something most people can only dream about."

Tyler ignored that, and instead focused on the revelation. "Who knows, Amy? You just might have been the difference. You might have been the one who put me over the top."

She stopped and turned to look deep into his eyes. "No, Tyler. You did that all by yourself."

Her simple, yet powerful degree of conviction left him silent for a time. She still didn't realize. She *had* been the difference. All that he pushed himself to achieve had begun on a mission trip to Pennsylvania years ago, with Amy at his side, a childhood friend he loved with wistfulness and an absolute, unabated longing. It was then that he had known for certain how his life would evolve: The power of his mission he would give to God—through music. The key to his heart, he would give only to Amy.

"You've always been there. Always. Don't ever doubt it."

Amy's lips twitched into a smile, and she sidled him a narrow-eyed glance. "Here's what else I know about you, beyond that well-deserved victory on *Opry Bound*. Most of it comes from CMT, but..." The way she parroted his words from their time on the boat made him smile. The crack about CMT made him laugh outright. "You have someone hot on your trail by the name of Kellen Rossiter. What's his deal? Who's

Kellen Rossiter?"

This was an unexpected turn in the direction of their conversation. It circled Tyler back to anxieties and the professional circumstances he had to resolve, with the fate of his career in the balance. "Rossiter's annoying."

"And flattering?"

Tyler huffed out a sound that didn't agree or disagree, but he forced himself to relax. He gave her a sidelong look. "Yeah. Admitting it makes me feel weak, but, yeah. I'm flattered by his attention. Dave Wells has me fully convicted on that count. Kellen is one of the biggest agents in the music industry. His roster is absolute A-List."

Amy paused. "And he's looking for you."

Tyler shrugged. "He got wind of the statistics for the new album and he's intrigued, that's all."

"Sure, because high-powered agents track every potential client, via any means necessary, when they're simply *intrigued*."

Tyler attempted to stifle a laugh, but in the end, he couldn't resist. They continued to walk, nearing the patio. "Sometimes, you're still a piece of sass, Amy."

"Sometimes? C'mon. What's the story? It seems to have you bugged. Why?"

"It's not that I'm bugged; it's that I'm afraid. He wants to represent me. Word I get from his numerous voicemails, e-mails, Facebook messages, Tweets, you name it…" This time it was Amy who burst out laughing. "…is that he's got his eye on me as a crossover artist."

That stopped her short once more, right at the lip of the patio. "Wow. It makes sense, but still. Wow."

Tyler wasn't as impressed. Not yet, anyway. "At

the sacrifice of the work I do for God, yeah. Wow." He eyed the large, padded chairs that were placed around a glass table, not wanting the moment to conclude. He'd do anything to stretch out the gift of this time with her, but she was probably tired, and… "You ready to go back in?"

She looked his way for a moment. "Not necessarily."

The grin he gave her was returned full-force, and they sat down.

"How would you be sacrificing the work you're doing for God by signing on with Kellen Rossiter?"

Tyler looked at thin, wispy clouds drifting across the light of a half-moon. Darkness increased by the second, adding an intimacy to the atmosphere. "Kellen is driven, and he's not afraid to push. If I sign on with him, I'll be pushed. I'm not sure how I feel about that. I don't want to get in over my head with a person who may not have all my best interests at heart. My life, my music, is a lot more than just making money and gaining audience exposure, know what I mean?"

Amy nodded. "In fact, I'd expect nothing less coming from you." She let a pause slip by. "But maybe Dave is right. Maybe you should at least talk to him. There's no harm in that."

"Yeah, you're right." Fast vanishing sunlight painted golden rays against the mauve, blue and pink colors of the sky. "I've already come to the conclusion that I'll regret it if I don't. It's just that I don't want to be led into the land of temptation. I'm meeting with him when I get back to Nashville, once the tour craziness is over with."

Amy studied him in silence for a moment. "Well, I know who and what you are. You'd never compromise. Not when it comes to the way you live your life."

A breeze rustled the leaves. She slumped comfortably, and closed her eyes as she rested her head against the back of the chair. "This place has the best vibe. I always feel at peace when I'm here. Content. Wish I always felt that way."

Tyler leaned forward, bracing his elbows on his knees while he watched her and absorbed. "Sounds like you've spent some time here." Her eyes remained closed, but her body went taut. Tyler instantly regretted the comment. "Sorry. I didn't mean to make you uncomfortable."

"No problem. It's tough. On one hand, I don't know what I'd do without Ken and Kiara. When I left Mark, I had nothing, Tyler. Literally nothing. I had the clothes on my back, and Pyper, which is all that mattered anyhow. Ken and Kiara let me stay here for a few months, until I found work, and was able to get an apartment and start a life of my own again."

"And on the other hand?"

She sighed, still never opening her eyes. She spoke in a low, quiet voice. "On the other hand I wish I hadn't made such stupid mistakes. I wish I hadn't needed to rely on them in the first place."

"What about your family? Your mom and dad?"

Amy turned her head, and at last looked at him. There was an ocean of pain in her eyes.

Tyler's brows pulled together.

"It's taken a while to find our way back."

A rift. Between Amy and her parents. Tyler remembered them—loving and devout, caring. Her statement earned his full attention. "They knew Mark was wrong for me. I wish I had listened to them. They were against our marriage from the get go, but when the pregnancy happened, there was no going back. We became alienated. Mark never wanted to be with them, so my visits became less and less frequent. Taking care of Pyper, protecting her, took every ounce of energy, every minute of time I had. They didn't give up exactly, they simply stepped back, and waited, and hoped. We're better now."

"But it wasn't the ending they hoped for you."

"Nope. Not at all. Emotionally, it was easier to crash here than with my parents. They wanted me, and Pyper, of course, but this was better. In all things, God works His good, right?"

Tyler didn't hesitate. "Yes."

He reached across the space between them and caressed her arm. At first, she seemed mesmerized by the play of his hand against her arm, so he kept his touch purposefully soft. Enticing. She stared, lost and dreamy, then her gaze lifted to his in transparent fascination.

That's when it happened. The epiphany.

The events of the day combined into a sudden and startling display; a stunning recognition hit him over the head, and slipped clean through to his heart. *He had an advantage here.* Loving emotion radiated from the one woman he had always wanted the most. He saw the longing in her eyes. He detected the faint trembling of her hands, the intense, heightened awareness that flowed between them—heated and electric.

But he'd be foolish if he didn't also recognize her fear, and the scars she carried from a failed marriage and the remnants of a broken heart trying hard to mend. No way would he move forward without extreme caution, and tender purpose.

Amy sat up. She stood more quickly than he would have expected, as though she were a bit nervous. "I should probably get Pyper home. I'm sure the excitement of the past few days is going to catch up with her before too long. I'll see you at services tomorrow, though. Ken tells me you'll be singing."

Tyler nodded and stood as well. Darkness moved in, deepening the shadows, draining away the day. That recognition stirred a heavy sadness. The end of their time together on his brief visit to Michigan inched inexorably closer, punctuated by his recognition of Amy's interest.

Maybe there was a way they could get together again, this time for longer than a weekend. In fact, he thought he knew just the way to make it happen. First, though, a couple weeks would have to pass in separation, to finish the tour. After that, he needed to resituate himself back home in Nashville and plan out his next steps—professionally, and now personally as well.

But for every night between now and then, he'd wonder if absence, however brief he intended it to be, would make her wounded but opening heart, grow even fonder.

8

Amy had never enjoyed services more. Naturally, Tyler's guest appearance had people crammed into every available space. Amy fell into the happiness of the service, rejoicing in the opportunity to absorb God's presence via prayer, Ken's preaching and Tyler's amazing music.

Afterwards, when she looked through the entry doors of the church, that euphoria and positivity took a nosedive. There, lined up outside the activity center, the tour buses waited, a convoy that would take Tyler back to his life on the road, and, ultimately, his home in Tennessee. Far from Michigan. Far from her. She bit her lower lip.

Suddenly, the beauty of yesterday's time together seemed like years ago.

"Mommy." Pyper tugged on her hand and Amy swallowed, blinking hard in an attempt to readjust herself.

"Yeah, sweetie?" She looked down, only to find Pyper regarding her intently. With concern.

"You gonnna cry?"

"No, Pyp. I'm fine."

"Mm'kay. You look sad." Amy could tell Pyper was nibbling on the inside of her cheek. "I thought maybe sayin' g'bye to Mr. Tyler might make you sad." Pyper peered toward Tyler who stood near the entrance of the church, surrounded by people. She was cautious, but something else rippled through Pyper's mood. Beneath the uncertainty, Amy sensed her daughter's affection, and longing to reach out. "We pro'bly should go see him, huh? Annie's over there with her mommy and daddy and everything."

Amy looked toward the swarm of people who engulfed Tyler. There was no way she'd get anywhere near him without a bulldozer. But she had to see him one last time. She needed to say goodbye, and thank him for giving her, and Pyper, such a sweet pair of days.

She stayed put, watching, and after a time, their eyes met. Amy gave him a tremulous smile but kept her distance for the time being. Tyler stood in place, his focus trained on her; his smile dawned. In short order, he did his best to politely disengage, nudging Ken and whispering. Ken glanced Amy's way and nodded, becoming a gentle buffer who interrupted conversations and redirected attention so Tyler could execute a smooth escape. They made a good team.

Amy caught his directing nod toward the rear corridor of the Narthex, near Ken's office. He took off promptly. Walking toward the group, Amy tagged up her daughter with Annie. "Would you mind keeping an eye on Pyper for just a few minutes?" she asked Kiara.

Kiara offered an understanding nod when Amy's gaze betrayed her, straying toward the doorway of Ken's office. Tyler had just gone inside. "Take your time," Kiara said in a tender voice.

Amy looked at her friend, feeling exposed. Uncertainty left her trembling. "I'll be right back."

Kiara smiled knowingly and ended their

conversation by turning to a parishioner who waited nearby.

Amy didn't think her walk down that straight stretch of a hallway would ever end.

She entered Ken's office and closed the door, not turning toward Tyler right away. What could be said, after all? Where could they realistically go from here, except to the land of farewell?

For the moment, she faced the door, clutching the cool, metal knob. A stirring of air alerted Amy to Tyler's approach. His hands came to rest on her shoulders. The motion was light, yet possessive in the best sense of the word. The warmth of his touch caused her to go still, close her eyes, and breathe deep. She folded her arms across her midsection; the moment lengthened and surrounded her completely.

"I hate to leave." His voice, the words, performed a tender caress. "There's still so much I want to say, and so much more I want to know."

"I feel the same way."

A weighted silence slid by, and at last she turned, facing Tyler, facing the inevitable. She relaxed her hold on herself, but her hands remained in tight fists at her sides. *Why?* she wanted to scream. *Why isn't my life ever easy? Why can't we be saying hello instead of goodbye?* She believed, believed absolutely, in the overriding goodness of God's plans. But at times like this, she sure did puzzle over what He could possibly be thinking.

Tyler studied her face, and stepped close, almost as though wanting to shield and protect her. She tipped her head back and looked into his eyes, not caring if he saw how much this moment hurt her, how much she cared, how much she now wished life had provided for a different outcome between the two of them.

Tyler regarded her steadily. "Give me your cell phone a sec."

Something in his features, that familiar warmth coupled with newfound intimacy, a compelling magnetism, made her catch her breath. She reached into her purse, and handed it over.

The intensity of the moment didn't end when he broke eye contact long enough to work his way into her list of contacts and start clicking keys. Her skin went warm as she waited, watching long, lean thumbs press and move. He paused, glanced at her in a considering way and then continued. When he finished, he snapped the phone shut and handed it over. He didn't release the device until her fingertips met up against his.

"I've added my phone…and my e-mail. Please use them, Amy. Please?" Amy trembled. His leaving stabbed through her spirit; she floundered, reality crashing in against wishes, and longing.

Valiantly, she shoved back the onslaught. "Turn around."

"Huh?"

"Turn around." Once he complied, she dropped her cell into its pocket and pulled a piece of paper and a pen from the depths of her oversized purse. Using his back as a surface, she began to write.

Tyler chuckled, and the sound let tingles loose against her skin. "This is so high school."

Amy stopped writing just long enough to peek at him around his shoulder. "High school was fun."

"Some of the time, yeah." He sidled her a look and his lips curved upward.

Finished, she gave him the small slip containing

her e-mail and cell number. "I'm not techno-savvy enough to enter in my contact information as fast as you just did, but I want to stay connected too, Tyler. Really."

With slow, careful motions, he folded the paper and slipped it neatly into the breast pocket of his shirt. "Amy?"

"Yeah?"

He looked at her intently for a moment. "This isn't high school. Not anymore."

He drew her in tight for a resistance-melting hug. *Tell me about it, Tyler. Tell me about it.* She let her world go soft. Her eyes fluttered closed, and for the first time in years, Amy remembered what it felt like to possess a yearning, loving heart that still believed in happily-ever-after, that still trusted, and still held fast to love's beauty and grace.

Tyler took both her hands in his. He stepped so close she could absorb his warmth. Placing their joined hands on his chest, he rested his forehead against hers.

Never, ever in her life—even in the throes of her crazy-mad longings for Mark Samuels—had Amy craved a kiss so badly. He was leaving. She just wanted a small, simple taste of him before he left.

In fact, that need overwhelmed her, transforming into tears that rolled slowly down her face as he leaned in, as she tilted toward him, ready. Waiting. But rather than claim her mouth, he slowly and tenderly brushed away her tears away with the slow glide of his cheek against hers. "Amy, I've dreamed of this moment for way too long. I don't want our first kiss to be a kiss goodbye."

The words rocked her world. She forced herself to focus, and look into his eyes. There she found the truth.

This moment, their reunion, was too precious to compromise. "I don't either," she admitted softly, hanging her head, weak with longing. "But we may never see…"

Tyler backed up and shook his head even harder. He lifted her chin and looked deep into her eyes, halting her words. He drew the pad of his thumb slowly, slowly against the line of her lower lip, and he blinked heavily. Then, his fingertips slipped beneath her tear-spiked lashes. "Yes, we will see each other again. I'm going to be bugging you."

"I give you permission," she answered, and she meant it…with all her heart.

"I want you to bug me back, OK? And, we'll see each other again soon. Count on it."

He was emphatic. Somehow, in the face of his sincerity, she found the tiniest measure of hope. It was thin and delicate but strong enough to help her hang on. And let him go.

So she nodded, and they held hands as Tyler opened the office door and they walked to the lobby. There, chaos reigned. Everyone at Woodland had lagged behind to wish Tyler and his crew a bon voyage. Beyond the now-open doors, the tour buses revved, belching diesel exhaust, engines rumbling. Doors squeaked as the drivers swung them open and tour members climbed aboard.

"Where will you be tonight?" Crazy, but she wanted to know, to have a connection to his whereabouts.

"Grand Rapids tonight, then Chicago for a few days afterward. Then we hit Columbus, Pittsburgh, and wrap up in Nashville."

Amy watched Pyper break away from Kiara and

Annie. Pyper stepped up slowly, taking Amy's hand, but her focus belonged to Tyler. "G'bye, Mr. Tyler," she said quietly. "Thank you for throwing me so good in the water."

"It was absolutely my pleasure." He crouched down, to Pyper's eye level. She backed away just slightly, tucking next to Amy's legs. Still, she smiled at him shyly. "I hope I see you again real soon, sugar beet."

Her smile went wider and she nodded, giving a soft giggle. "Sugar beet," she repeated, and giggled again. "I'm a sugar beet?"

Tyler gave her arm a gentle squeeze. "Yep. You're sweet, just like a sugar beet."

She gave a little wave. "Bye."

Tyler tweaked her nose lightly, and stroked her cheek. "See you soon."

Now, he focused on Amy. "Remember. We're gonna stay connected."

"I promise to reach out, if you do, too. I don't want to lose you."

"You won't, Amy. You *won't*."

She fought against tears once more, already aching with the pain of missing him. Pretty much a ridiculous reaction, Amy thought, since they had been reunited for less than forty-eight hours. Tyler's rock-solid embrace trembled a bit, but he held her tight and sure. Amy sighed, an involuntary reaction to breathing in the subtle aroma of his earthy, appealing cologne, savoring the way his arms felt, locked securely around her waist.

She wanted to believe him. He lifted a hand to her cheek, stroked it as though revering a treasure. Fire lit her skin, blooming through her body, a fire stoked by the sureness of being in his arms, sharing with him, simply being with him.

But her mind worked in direct contradiction to her heart, warning her, sounding off alarm bells and raising flags.

He's Tennessee; you're Michigan. He's a celebrity; you're barely on your feet again. You've devoutly guarded your heart from further harm, yet you fall for him so easily. This is absolutely crazy.

In the end, all of her arguments did nothing to alter one key truth: being with Tyler again felt good. And right.

9

"Pyper, you got a package in the mail." And it was postmarked Tennessee. That made Amy's lips curve.

"I did? What is it, Mommy?" Pyper bounded from her room, where she and Lucy Robbins, a friend from down the street, were playing with fashion dolls.

"D'no, honey. I think it's from Tyler."

Pyper's eyes went wide, her smile large and just a little shy. "Really?" She took the thick, insulated envelope in eager hands and plunked her bottom down on the couch so she could tear into it. Lucy came out of Pyper's bedroom, drawn by the commotion.

Amy thumbed through the rest of the Saturday offerings. A glossy set of advertisements, a pair of bills—nothing nearly as exciting as Pyper's delivery.

"Wow!" Upon hearing Pyper's happy shout, Amy set the mail on the living room end table and joined her daughter on the couch.

"What is it?" Lucy asked, crowding her friend to see what Pyper uncovered.

"Color books, and a big picture book, too—with mountains! An' he sent me playing cards and stickers, too!"

Amy grinned. Tyler had sent Pyper all kinds of stuff native to Tennessee. A thick coloring book was all about Nashville, and another one about the Smoky Mountains. The third item was a hardback, coffee table book with pictures and information about the state. On the cover of that one, Amy noticed a bright blue sticky note.

Pyper turned to Lucy, a happy set to her features. "This is from Mr. Tyler. He's a friend of me and my mommy, and he's a really good singer. He's on the radio and stuff, and he throws real good in the water, too." Pyper ended her litany of Tyler's traits just long enough to point to the sticky note. "Mommy, what's this?"

Upon it was scrawled the words, *Amy, Open me. ASAP.*

Puzzled, and intrigued, Amy took custody of the book. "I think that one's for me, snug-a-bug."

"Mm'kay." Enthused, Pyper scooped up her prizes and grabbed Lucy's hand; she was flushed with pleasure, and that tickled the sides of Amy's heart. "C'mon, Lucy. You can color in them with me."

Off they charged. Left in peace, Amy opened the book. Inside the front cover, she found a folded sheet of letter-sized paper that she opened promptly.

Her breath caught. Her jaw dropped open and she launched from the couch, scrambling to grab her cell phone. She scrolled fast for Tyler's name.

When he answered, there was no greeting, no preamble, just the sound of his soft, musical laughter. "Le'me guess. You just got the mail."

Amy's laughter bubbled over. "Yes, I did."

"And? So? You in?" His eager excitement rolled through the connection.

"Tyler! You can't even be *halfway* serious about this."

"D'ya wanna bet?" His teasing tones went serious. "I know my proposal may be tough to execute, with

107

your work schedule and all, but I'm missin' you. I really want to try to get together, sooner rather than later if you can swing it…"

His words trailed off and he waited. Amy let herself fall into the moment, and breathe. The printed sheet she held detailed a one-week trip, for her and Pyper, to Tennessee. The itinerary, coordinated by a travel agency in Franklin, was marked "Draft" with travel dates yet to be determined.

"Nothing is set in stone. You can pick whatever dates you want, but nothing changes the intent. I want you and Pyper to take a taste of my life here in Tennessee."

Amy couldn't begin to wrap her head around the idea, or summon a proper response without careful thought and consideration. After all, this involved Pyper as well.

"It's all on the up-and-up. Let me know when you're coming and my aunt will stay with us for the week. Call her a chaperone of sorts. All I know is this: I want you and Pyper here, as soon as you can manage. I miss my girls."

His girls. Amy braced herself against futility, thinking, *Oh, Tyler, if only.*

Still, the sound of his voice wrapped around her, and she savored its inflections and rich, deep warmth. His love saturated her, fed her craving heart with miraculous, life-giving food that came to her spirit as nothing less than a benediction from God. "I wish…"

"What? What do you wish?"

"I wish I could just let go, and say yes, but I'm afraid. I'm afraid for what the end of this whole thing would mean, for me, and for Pyper. I can't afford to be risky with my life, and my emotions, or Pyper will pay the price just as dearly as me."

He sighed, but not out of anger, or disappointment. Amy knew that at once. "I know, but don't deny me the pleasure of being able to do things for you. There's so much inside of me I want to give you."

"Can you give me a day or two to think this over, and see what I can do?"

"I'll give you even more if you need it. Like I said, the dates are flexible, the idea is a constant."

She allowed a tender laugh at that. "Understood, and appreciated—on both counts. Tyler, this is amazing, please don't think I'm hesitating to be coy, or difficult, or—"

"Amy, don't diminish how well I know you by even saying such a thing. I understand exactly where you're coming from. And let me reassure you again— my aunt would stay with us when you and Pyper come to visit. This isn't untoward; it's about giving ourselves a chance to build on something. Something special. So, think it over and let me know when...not if...you can make it out here, OK?"

Safe enough, and fair enough. Nothing would give her more pleasure than spending time with Tyler again, and he was going to such effort to make sure she was cared for on every level.

For the first time in five dry, stagnant years, Amy actually recognized herself as being precious. God had to be at work, bringing Tyler back into her life.

Amy stroked the phone, tucking it almost lovingly against her cheek. He was at the other end. He was present and faithful to the promises he had made before leaving Michigan. They had both made sure to reestablish their old ties, and in the week and a half since his departure, they had e-mailed, shared text updates, and chatted on the phone regularly.

"OK. Let me check in at work and see how quickly I can get away from Edwards Construction. I'm not going to kid you, it may be a little dicey. It's spring into summer, work is ramping up. I don't want to pull the rug out from under JB."

"I understand completely. Keep me posted."

"Deal. I will. And Tyler?

"Yeah, honey?"

"Thank you. Thank you for making Pyper so happy, and for being so wonderful, to both of us."

"That comes to me as easy as breathing, Amy. See you," he concluded with emphasis.

She smiled, her heart tripping with expectation, and a dangerous level of hope. "See you," she replied softly, but with equal conviction.

She ended the call and stared straight ahead, seeing nothing whatsoever, as the ramifications set in. Her mind began to spin with plans and ideas. From here, there were only two places Amy could think of to turn: first prayer, and then Kiara.

❧❦

"Why, Kiara? Why am I being so completely reckless? Don't you think I'm being reckless?"

After Sunday services the next day, Amy visited with her friend in the Youth Formation offices at Woodland Church.

Amy leaned against the arm of the chair, cradling her head. "Do you have any idea how often I've thought of Pennsylvania?"

"I'll bet. Tyler's return kind of brought it all back,

didn't it?"

Amy chose to let that observation, and its double entendre, go. "I remember, back then, when you told me to pay more attention to the man who treated me well rather than the one who would rule the basketball courts, and the court of popularity."

They sat next to each other at a small, round conference table. Kiara nodded, and Amy could have even sworn she heard her sigh softly. "I remember that conversation, too. You've always been so bright and positive and magnetic. You draw people in by virtue of your beauty—inside and out. At the time, you couldn't help how you felt—about both of them."

"You're being way too easy on me."

"No, I understand exactly where you're coming from, and what led you to the choices you've made."

Amy sighed, her heart aching when she looked at her friend. "I never, ever should have refused that piece of wisdom, Kiara. You came by your knowledge through hard knocks. I should have paid better attention and learned from you. It would have saved me so much grief and regret. I made a mess of my life. I'm ashamed of what I let happen, and all my stupid decisions."

In a gesture of compassion, and understanding, Kiara reached across the tabletop and rested her hand on top of Amy's. "Whoa back a second, and slow down. Don't take the brunt of the hit, here. You weren't the one who abused, you were the victim. And when you're young, it's so hard to absorb the larger truth—that life always plays the equalizer. After all, look at the difference between Mark and Tyler now that high school and teen influences are past." Kiara leaned forward. "That said, I want you to remember one other very important fact. God uses everything for the good. Everything. After all, if you had made different choices, you wouldn't have Pyper. Right?"

The statement stopped Amy's self-centered thought pattern like a brick wall. The shock of Kiara's words sank in deep and rippled through her system. "Ye...yeah..."

"*Yeah.* God, my darling girl, is now giving you an open door. Offering up a second chance. You're being directed toward a new road to explore with someone who's adored you from the moment he met you. And isn't it ironic? The quiet, shy boy you knew back then has evolved into a handsome, charismatic, talented man. He's become the kind of man you probably always dreamed of being with as the popular young girl who was the life of the party back in high school. The boy you knew needs to be reconciled to the man he is now. Because I tell you true, Tyler Brock is as swept away by you now as he ever was in high school." Kiara arched a brow in challenge and provocation. "Think you can handle that, Miss Thing?"

Amy nibbled her lower lip. She fingered the worn edges of her bible, the well cared for, but much used black leather book her current focal point. Just before seeing Kiara, she had touched base with her boss, Jeremy Edwards, letting him know she might need to take a week off in the very near future. He had seemed interested, and even agreeable; Amy promised to let him know more about it on Monday morning.

For now, it seemed, all signs pointed to Tennessee.

Foot traffic and chatter faded the longer they sat together. Parishioners left Woodland. Soon, Ken would probably stop by, looking for his wife. The idea made Amy sigh wistfully on the inside, longing for a life that featured the love, and devotion, of a wonderful man. Still, everything remained uncertain. "And after the week is finished? What about then? The facts remain. He's a celebrity; I'm most definitely not. His life, is far from mine, and then there's the whole uprooting thing."

Kiara puzzled. "Uprooting thing?"

"Um-Hmm. Let's play the fantasy card for a moment. We have a great time together. We decide to build a future together. That future, for Tyler, won't be in Michigan. His home is down south now, and as for me, well, during the past year, I've done nothing but drag myself, and Pyper, all over creation in an attempt to rebuild our lives. We're getting back on track again. I don't want to ruin that progress by yanking both of us away from everything we know, and everything that's familiar."

Kiara's lips curved into a grin, then blossomed into a smile. "Know what this reminds me of?"

"What?"

"The story of Ruth and Boaz. Honestly, the book of Ruth is my favorite. It's full of such upheaval, yet so much tender loving mercy and romantic devotion."

The point struck Amy's soul like a well-aimed arrow. She tilted her head, wondering where Kiara was headed with that comment.

"You make valid points about abandoning the life you've known here in Detroit. But in the end, the answers you're looking for depend on you and Tyler. Listen to what I have to say, Amy, and think about it. Take it deeply to heart. Faith is a risk. Faith always requires trust. Faith requires vulnerability and absolute belief that, despite everything, God leads you to goodness. I honestly and truly believe Tyler has reentered your life for a reason. As part of a plan. Figure out where to take it, and I think happiness will follow. Just like Ruth and Boaz. It won't be easy, but it'll be so worth it."

Amy went flush, prickly and expectant. She realized, for the first time in years, that there was happiness, and joy, to be found, if she could just let go and embrace it. Could she? Could she trust herself again, like she used to in her youth?

"All I know is I want to try," Amy swallowed hard, banishing the tightness in her throat. "I'm so sick of this hole in my chest. It hurts so much."

"Then fill it up. Fill it up by recognizing God's grace, by recognizing the love you feel. It's the only way that hole you're talking about will ever get repaired."

10

Amy held fast to Pyper's hand as they skittered down the jet way to their waiting plane. Pyper glowed with excitement, pulling hard on Amy's arm. They entered the cabin, welcomed by a lovely female flight attendant who gave Pyper a wink. "Welcome aboard. Enjoy your flight to Nashville."

Amy's heart raced.

Pyper beamed. "Mommy, this is so cool! I can't wait to fly! I'm so *excited*!"

Tyler had purchased first class tickets, so their seats were close to the nose of the plane. Pyper shimmied her arms free of her backpack, which was stuffed full of necessities like the coloring books Tyler had provided, a couple of stuffed animals, some crayons of course, and a pair of her newer fashion dolls, complete with clothing changes. She claimed her seat, right next to the window, instantly fascinated by the arrival of the luggage trolley. Amy buckled in, already grateful for the wide, comfortable seats. While she pushed a canvas tote into the storage space in front of her feet, Pyper likewise stowed her backpack. Pyper tucked her hands beneath her thighs as she swung her legs back and forth. Her smile burst across her face like a heavenly light. She wore a simple, flowered sundress and sandals, her hair a wavy cloud of deep blonde around her face and shoulders. Amy had opted for white capris, and an aqua blouse, worn open over a white silk shell. Her belt was a converted scarf full of pastel swirls. Yes, she admitted to herself, she had fussed for Tyler.

"When will we be there?"

"In a couple of hours."

"But you said it'll be weird—that the time changes."

"Yep. Nashville is an hour behind Michigan. It's nine o'clock here, but it's only eight o'clock where Tyler lives. We arrive in Nashville at 9:40."

Pyper visually puzzled, then shrugged. "Weird."

Pyper's energy and overflow of exuberance only fed Amy's nervous, but happy outlook about the trip to come.

A male flight attendant, dressed in a crisp blue uniform stopped by their seats. "Would you like something to drink, ladies?"

Pyper shrank back a bit, nesting as close to Amy as she could in a body-warmed request for reinforcement. Amy smiled at her daughter, tucking an arm around her. "Want some orange juice?"

Pyper looked into her eyes and nodded. "Orange juice for two, please."

The man returned a short time later with a treat for Pyper. He had mixed a bit of sparkling tonic water with Pyper's juice and added a maraschino cherry that floated on top. "This is a specialty of our airline. We're asking our most special passengers to try it. Can you tell me what you think?"

Blinking, still ducking by Amy's side, Pyper accepted the ice-filled plastic tumbler and took a sip. She smacked her lips and her eyes went wide. "It's awesome!"

"I'm so glad you like it. Here's another treat for being our official beverage sampler today. It makes you an honorary part of our crew." He handed Pyper a plastic-wrapped set of wings.

"Thank you ve'y much." Pyper tilted her head and fluttered her lashes at the attendant.

"You're more than welcome. Enjoy your flight!"

"Mm'kay. I will." He started to walk away. Pyper leaned forward, tracking him. "An' if you want any other drinks tested, I'll do it for you."

Amy stifled a charmed laugh, diverting her reaction by kissing the top of Pyper's head. Their flight steward grinned as well.

Minutes later, they were soaring, and Amy couldn't stop thinking about what awaited her at the other end of this voyage. Kiara's comments about Ruth and Boaz had stuck with her, working through her with a resounding sense of God's promise when it comes to love. She had read through the Book of Ruth twice since their conversation, renewed by the tender shoots of Ruth's hope and unshakable faith, by Boaz's demonstrative affection, his compassion and protection.

The Book of Ruth, with its message of love and an intimate mercy, spoke to a chamber in her soul that remained, since her divorce, in desperate need. Even now, as she embraced the comfort of a deluxe flight, as she slid deeper into Tyler's care with every mile that passed, a tingling quiver went wild in her belly; a dance of sparks lit her senses. Her entire body went flush, radiant at the mere thought of the one who was already giving her, and Pyper, a world full of blessings.

಄಄

Hand-in-hand with Pyper, Amy made her way through the airport and down an escalator towards the baggage claim where Tyler had agreed to meet them. She found the turnstile for their flight and while she waited for the conveyor belt to begin churning, she punched in the auto-dial connection to Tyler's cell phone.

"Baggage claim five, right?" he said instead of the standard hello.

Amy laughed. A flood of goose bumps danced against her skin, building her sense of anticipation. "Tyler Brock, ladies and gentlemen. He's not just a talented musician. He's also psychic." The rumble of his laughter made her so happy. "Are you here yet?"

"Close."

An instant later, the slightly roughened touch of a man's fingertips slid against her hand from behind, slowly removing the cell phone from her grasp and disengaging the call.

Amy spun, delight filling her as Tyler performed a quick and tempting nuzzle against her neck. "Welcome to Nashville," he murmured into her ear.

He wore a pair of faded blue jeans and a nondescript blue sweatshirt. A baseball cap was turned backwards, sunglasses dangled from his fingertips. He may have been attempting to blend and sink beneath notice, but Amy's heart beat erratically. She looked up at him and smiled, her emotions exposed to the core. Tyler slid an arm around her waist and gave her a squeeze, but then he let go so he could squat down and say hello to Pyper.

"How's my sugar beet?" He didn't reach out or

pull her toward him. Instead, he kept his distance and simply smiled into her eyes.

"I fine," she answered quietly, holding tightly to Amy's side. "How're you?"

Tyler's smile only grew. "I'm doing a whole lot better now that you and your mommy are here to visit. My aunt, RuthAnne, can't wait to meet you. She's already planning a lunch spread. You hungry?"

Pyper took a small inch toward being receptive. "Sorta. I helped the people on the plane test out how good their soda drinks were."

"Amazing!"

Chuckling, Amy stroked a hand against Pyper's hair. "I think taking her maiden voyage in first class spoiled her for anything less." Amy gave her daughter's shoulder a gentle squeeze. "Can you show Tyler your wings?"

"Mmm-hmm. Here." She stayed glued to Amy's side, but rifled through the pocket of her dress and found what she was after. Tyler admired the plastic toy wings she handed over that bore the logo of the airline.

An alarm sounded and a few seconds later, the rotator belt of the baggage conveyor came to life. Not long after, their two suitcases were in Tyler's hands, and he led the way to an adjoining parking garage. "I'm right over here."

Tyler pointed his key fob. After a chirp of the security system and a brief flash of the rear lights, Amy realized which car was his, and her eyes went wide. It was a fire engine red Ford Mustang.

Convertible.

Even Pyper was awestruck. "Mr. Tyler, that's a really cool car!"

"Oh, Pyper, you're a Detroit girl. You know better

than anyone that this isn't a mere car. This is a work of art on wheels."

Pyper burst out laughing. "That's not true! It doesn't even got a picture frame!"

"Know what? You're right, it doesn't, especially when I open up the roof. You guys game for some wind in your hair, and some sunshine?"

"Yeah!" Amy and Pyper answered in unison.

Tyler stowed luggage, then joined them next to the car. Amy's eyes went wide when she saw that he carried a booster seat. "You honestly thought of a booster seat? I'm officially amazed...I have to admit, I was a little worried, but of course, I didn't even think of it until we had boarded the plane."

Tyler went about setting up the child restraint in the back seat. "I'd love to take credit, but this is all RuthAnne. She has grandkids, and knew enough to let me know I'd need it. She had an extra one she's letting me borrow for the week."

Being in the care of an inherently thoughtful man caused Amy's delight to bubble and flow, for she had nearly forgotten what such a thing was like. Her gaze locked with Tyler's, and she hoped her eyes reflected her appreciation.

Once they were settled, he retracted the top of the vehicle. At the first stoplight outside of the airport, he draped a wrist over the steering wheel and turned toward her. "You look fantastic. I'm so glad you're here."

"Me, too."

He leaned in. She watched him do so with wide eyes, trembling with the expectation of his mouth gliding against hers. She imagined his textures, and flavors. But then Tyler paused, and chuckled softly.

His breath skimmed warm against her skin when he tilted her head slightly and gave her cheek a tender nuzzle, just like he had in baggage claim. She tilted her head, turned, beset by the sweetest cloud of wanting…seeking his lips…but Tyler moved smoothly away, a grin lighting his eyes. . "More on that later," he murmured.

The light went green, but she wanted his kiss, literally ached for it. Shaking her head, Amy worked free of languor and focused on the road ahead. Once they cleared out of Nashville, heading south on I-65, they sped through rolling land dotted by large trees and crowned by expansive homes.

Half an hour later, Tyler pulled down a gravel road that curved through a thick stand of sycamore and magnolia trees. At the end came her first view of his home.

It was a farmhouse of deep yellow with large windows that shone in the sun. A wide, wrap-around porch framed in the lower level. Towering old trees stood sentinel. Dark green evergreen shrubs, a variety of brightly colored flowers and ground covering phlox in pink, white, and purple completed the welcoming landscape. A few of the large windows, she now noticed, were edged by stained glass squares that captured the light as they drove up. The overall effect was an invitation to homey comfort with the added touch of southern charm and warmth.

Tyler slowed the car and pulled close to a set of wooden stairs that led to the front door. This was exactly the kind of place she had imagined for him. When he parked, Amy turned, and found him already watching her.

"Tyler, this is gorgeous."

"I like it, too!" Pyper looked around eagerly, already itching to explore, Amy could tell.

They filed out of the car; as they unloaded the trunk, the front door came open and a tall, attractive woman of middle age stepped onto the porch, smiling a greeting.

"Hey, RuthAnne." Tyler paused to give her a wave.

"There y'all are!" RuthAnne Newman was slim and lean, her gray hair fashioned into a loose bunch at the nape of her neck. "So, I finally get to meet Amy and Pyper! Come on in! Y'hungry?"

"I am!" Pyper drew up the straps of her backpack while Amy took custody of her tote and purse. Tyler claimed their luggage and carried it inside.

"Then let's eat! How was your flight?"

There wasn't a formal or stuffy vibration to be found here. Amy liked RuthAnne instantly, drawn by the older woman's sweet graciousness. Simple jeans and a t-shirt added to RuthAnne's aura of comfortable appeal. In the kitchen, serving platters filled with deli meats, cheeses, and bread, a platter of fruit and a bowl of chips, plates and utensils and a tall, crystal pitcher full of lemonade were laid out.

Amy's mouth watered. Pyper looked at RuthAnne with the sweetest expression on her face. "Thank you for this."

"Oh!" RuthAnne seemed genuinely touched. "Well you are a peach, aren't ya?"

Pyper giggled. "No. I'm a sugar beet. That's what Tyler says."

No *Mr.* Tyler this time. Amy sent Tyler a knowing look, but kept quiet. Tyler, however, smiled widely. Another slow, sure, step forward as formalities vanished. But Pyper had yet to truly relax around him, and completely let down her guard.

Time, Amy thought to herself. *Time and stabilizing influences will have to work out Pyper's fears.*

"The thanks go double for me, RuthAnne," Amy said. "This looks wonderful."

"I'm happy to do it. Tyler's been awfully excited about you finally gettin' here."

Tyler cleared his throat and shuffled in a manner that touched Amy's heart.

After lunch, Tyler took them on a tour of the house. A great room stretched across the bulk of the lower level. It was elegant—just leaning toward formal—but that formality was tempered nicely by country-style touches like a large wreath of dried wild flowers that decorated the space above the fireplace, brass lamps with simple white shades, braided area rugs, and an overstuffed sofa and loveseat. A nearby rocker, with a brimming brass magazine rack to its left, was comfortably padded and draped by a crocheted afghan.

Next came a large den/music room, where Amy spied his music awards, and a framed platinum record for his latest release. Pride and awe tickled her fingertips as she lightly stroked the surface. A grand piano and half dozen guitars were stationed throughout. A stack of blank sheet music rested atop the piano bench. On the instrument's music stand were additional pages. These sheets featured filled in staves complete with hand-written notes, and what looked like lyrics in progress. An image of Tyler at work in this space came to life in Amy's mind. What was he working on? What would come next? She longed to step up, and explore, but instead followed the lead of their host.

Upstairs, Tyler showed them to their rooms. At their first stop, he allowed Pyper to walk in first. "Pyper, you get your choice. Do you want to stay with your mama here in this room, or do you want to see the room I thought you might enjoy?"

She looked a bit doubtful. "Can I...like...sorta wait and see?"

"Sure you can," Tyler assured.

Amy's room featured a king-sized sleigh bed with a quilted down comforter of white that looked like a cloud. Sunshine yellow walls were sponge painted with dabs of blue, and crank-style windows were wide open to the gorgeous summer day.

Pyper's room came next. It featured a four-poster bed with tied-back netting. A cherry wood desk filled space beneath the open window with curtains that rippled in a soft breeze. "This is so pretty!" Pyper walked in, and gasped.

"I hoped you'd like it. And even if you don't sleep here, there're some things I got for you to play with, and you're free to hang out here any time."

Pyper shuffled through the room, taking note of a fresh stack of coloring books, a supply of blank paper, and an open box of markers. Small puzzle boxes dotted the top of a long dresser and there was also a large plastic ball and a mesh bag that held a pail, a trowel, a spade and a pair of small, flowered gardening gloves.

"I always wanted to play with flowers." Pyper lifted up the tools and looked them over.

"I sure could use your help with that." Tyler stepped up and explored the gardening bag along with Pyper. "I've got yard work to do now that I'm all done with the tour."

She turned to him. "Maybe...could I stay with my mommy tonight, and then see about being here after?"

"Sugar beet, you can do whatever you want."

They finished settling in, and then Tyler took them for a walk. Amy discovered he owned quite a spread of land, bordered by white wooden rail fences. There was simply no way to stay closed up and tense in such a perfect setting, which, Amy imagined, was precisely why he purchased it.

That evening, Amy tucked in her exhausted daughter. Pyper had been existing on excess adrenaline for hours. After prayers, and a promise to join her shortly, Amy left the bedroom behind, but not before cracking open the door slightly so the room would be bathed in the pale illumination of the hall light.

She returned downstairs. In passing, she noted Tyler was on the telephone in the landing, and he gave her an apologetic look during a pause in the conversation. Amy just smiled at him and gave him a wink. In the living room, RuthAnne rocked peaceably, watching a game show on television as she cross-stitched.

The domesticity appealed to Amy, as did the quiet, homey comfort of being in Tyler's home. Strolling toward the entryway, she pushed open the screen door and decided to enjoy the front porch.

A pair of cylindrical hanging lamps poured buttery, yellow light across comfortably worn floorboards. Amy sat on the thick padded cushions of a swing that was suspended from the porch ceiling by sturdy metal chains. Wicker chairs and tables were positioned close by, and hurricane lamps dotted the window ledges and tables. There was a box of matches within reach, so Amy lit them and settled back to enjoy the flickering glow.

After an early start this morning, and the stress of making sure everything was set for the trip, she felt a bit rumpled, but being with Tyler again reinvigorated her spirit. She leaned her head back and closed her eyes. For a soothing length of time, she absorbed the scent of spring-kissed air, the caress of the soft, warm breeze that glossed her skin. Incrementally her body unwound and relaxed.

"Hey there."

Amy turned, watching Tyler set a mug of tea on the wicker table next to her. "Hey there yourself." She delivered a sheepish grin. "I think I've discovered my favorite part of your house. This is a wonderful spot. "

"It's my favorite, too."

Tyler sat next to her, propping a booted foot against the edge of the large wicker table positioned before them. Pushing slightly, he set the swing into a slow, lulling motion. The black bowl of a sky was sprinkled with stars, lit by a half-moon. The only interruption in the view came from rolling mountain peaks, the valley lights curving upward against the ridge basin.

"Sorry about the call. I didn't mean to be rude."

"Don't even worry about it. Is everything all right?"

"Fine." Something strange rode beneath the surface of that too-fast reply. "So is my sugar beet all tucked in?"

"She is. Happily exhausted, too. Just like me."

"Good. On both counts."

Amy kept quiet for a time, but remained watchful, savoring the joyful nuance of being in this moment, with Tyler, on such a beautiful night. Since Tyler kept them in motion, she drew up her legs and wrapped her arms around them, tucking against the side of the swing so she faced him. "You're a busy man. Even in the off-tour season. Was it an important call?"

He stretched his arm across the back of the swing and stroked her cheek with his knuckles, giving her a smile. "Amy, know what I love about this? It feels like only five minutes ago that I hugged you goodbye after the mission trip to Pennsylvania, or said goodbye to you a couple weeks ago in Detroit. It's like we're just now picking up the threads of a conversation that never ended. I wish you knew how much I love that aspect of our relationship."

She went warm, and smiled at him brightly. "I know what you mean. Now answer the question."

They swung, and Tyler paused a moment, seeming to take a few beats of time to form his words. Amy studied his profile.

"I'm planning to take y'all to Rutledge Falls and Fall Creek tomorrow, but I've got an eight o'clock meeting in town to contend with first. Our Tennessee tour will be my reward for enduring it."

"Town meaning Nashville?"

"Kellen Rossiter. I was going to meet with him last week, but I ended up having to reschedule. That was him on the phone. He wants to meet for breakfast beforehand. Kind of an informal pre-meeting to make things a bit more personal and friendly."

Tyler sighed heavily, and all at once, Amy came aware of the reasons behind his nervous, unsettled attitude. He was still worried about the potential for selling out. Crossing over mounted monumental pressures upon him.

"I swear. The most difficult thing to contend with

is the whole atmosphere of the entertainment industry. I love making music. I love sharing God's truth through the songs I sing. I truly do. Nothing else compares to it."

"Because it's your calling." Giving a nod, she reached for her tea to take a sip. Mint flavor swirled, and burst on her tongue.

"True enough, but the people I see every day? They're not my crowd. I hate that terrible sense of aggression and the self-centeredness of the entertainment industry. And, not to belabor the point, since we already hashed it out back in Detroit, but I just can't get a bead on this guy. I admit that's got me nervous. I can usually gauge people pretty well. Not this time. This time, I'm confused, and I'm still not sure where God means for me to go with the opportunities Kellen is presenting."

"You never had an agent?" That surprised Amy. Somehow she assumed they would have beaten a pathway to Tyler's doorway.

"I never needed one. When I won *Opry Bound*, I had plenty of offers, but I had a guaranteed contract with Exclamation Point Records. They took good care of me on album number one, and gave me lots of room to create on record number two, so I didn't see a need. But, maybe now the time is right to sign on with some representation. Not out of greed, or a need for *more*, but to insure I'm making the most of the opportunities I'm being given."

"Opportunities you've *earned*," she amended tenderly. "And part of the purpose of performing, and sharing your gift is to gain exposure to more people. There's no shame in that, Tyler."

"No, there isn't, on the surface, anyway. I do want

to grow as an artist, and help more people discover the message in my music." Tyler seemed to think about that for a moment.

"Pray."

That single stronghold of a word drew his gaze to hers, but Amy could still see a hint of hesitation in his eyes. "I don't mean for that to be a pat, simplistic answer to what you're going through," she said. "I believe it's the only way you'll find your way through, and keep on track with what God wants for you."

"I agree. Completely. I *have* been praying. Trouble is, the confusion doesn't go away. God knows, from the depths of my heart, I don't want to mess this up, but I just can't figure out what to do yet. I'm not feeling the answers yet. I'm not sure of God's pathway right now."

"Then you're not supposed to. God knows what you're up against. He'll give you the discernment you need, the comfort you're looking for, but for now he's obviously telling you to rest in faith, and trust Him."

"I know. I'm trying. But the world I'm pulling closer to? I'm not going to lie to you, Amy, it scares me."

"And that's understandable. Plus, Kellen Rossiter is so much a part of that whole scene you're probably not sure of his motives, and if they'll serve you well."

"That sums it up." They shared a smile, and Amy drank a bit more of her tea. She wrapped her fingers around the warm mug and savored the spicy aroma of the rising steam. "I don't want to fall into a guitar-string style of faith and morality."

Amy couldn't help it. The analogy caused her to bubble up with laughter. "Excuse me? A guitar-string style morality?"

"Yeah. You know. Variable. Conforming to our needs instead of God's plan." He held up an imaginary air guitar, pretending to fiddle with it. "Oh, I like this a lot. I think I'll tighten it up a little here. Hmm...don't like that so much. It's hard, and doesn't feel so good. No problem. I'll just loosen up that next string and make it all work." Tyler shrugged, resuming their swinging motion by pushing gently against the table. "It's all about making things what you want them to be, forcing them into place by stubborn will and pride instead of paying attention to God's overall symphony. Know what I mean?"

Boy, did she. Amy nodded. "Leaning on our own understanding."

"Exactly." Tyler didn't hide his unease at the idea. "Biggest pitfall there is, especially in the entertainment industry. People start reading, and believing, their own press releases, and start thinking they know better than God. Or, worse yet, think they're on a par with God. It's such an easy trap to fall into. I'm trying to avoid it, but—"

"But then along comes an amazing opportunity to minister in an even bigger way and move forward with what you love. Music."

"Yeah."

"Starting tomorrow."

Tyler chuckled, but the sound lacked any degree of humor. "Starting tomorrow."

On impulse, she reached out and gave his fingertips a tight, reassuring squeeze meant to convey her support and faith in his strength of spirit.

God, she prayed in silence, *thank you. Thank you for this wonderful, Christ-centered man whose mission in life is to spread your love. Please. Please, dear Lord. Take care of him for me. With my past history, with the abuse and horrors I've endured, I still don't see a future for us as a couple. I feel like I'd bring him down. I'd never survive the glare of a public spotlight, and either would Pyper. I can't yank my daughter into a whole new life at this tender point in her development. But, all that aside, he's precious. Guard him. Be with him tomorrow.*

11

At just after seven the next morning, Tyler left his home. Amy, Pyper and Aunt RuthAnne were sound asleep within. He, on the other hand, had barely closed his eyes all night. Tension slid through him. Nervous anxiety thumped at his spirit, giving him too much energy, too many things to think about.

Purposely early, he made his way into the heart of Nashville and parked on 5th Avenue, not far from their chosen restaurant: 417 Union. The block or two he needed to walk would do him good, and hopefully help him settle before the meeting. He was shown to a booth positioned toward the front of the restaurant. It was then that Tyler rested his fidgeting hands, closed his eyes, bowed his head, and repeatedly prayed a simple, three-word petition: *Discernment, Lord. Please.*

Tyler heard the door squeak open. Footsteps sounded. Reflex left him wanting to lift his head to see who entered the restaurant. He rebuked the reaction, but his prayers drifted to silence.

"Good morning, Mr. Rossiter. How are you?" When Tyler heard the greeting, he sucked in a deep, smooth breath, still diverting his eyes, forcing anxiety to take a back seat to God's prompting and direction.

"I'm great, Janie, thank you."

"Your party is here, and seated."

"I see him. Thanks again."

"My pleasure."

The simple exchange of pleasantries finally roused Tyler. With a restored sense of calm, he greeted Kellen's approach. "You're a regular here."

Kellen took the seat across from Tyler and gave a laugh. "Guilty. This place roped me in a couple years ago with their prime rib hash."

Tyler winced. "Something about the word 'hash'...."

Kellen laughed again. "Give their French toast platter a try. It runs a close second."

They perused menus for a few moments while their waitress introduced herself and delivered iced water. Tyler desperately needed his morning coffee fix, so he ordered that promptly. Kellen went for a tall orange juice.

"I meant to ask you," Kellen began, spreading a white linen napkin across his lap. "You going to the Exclamation Point party on Friday?"

Tyler nodded. He wondered if Amy would be interested in attending his record label's annual publicity push. They could make a full, fun evening of it. Otherwise, he'd make an appearance, and return home as soon as possible. Nothing superseded Amy and Pyper's visit. "Yeah. I plan to be there."

"Good. Me, too."

"You seem to be making more and more inroads with Christian artists."

"Let's just say I'm *trying*." A pointed look was tempered by the curve of his lips.

Tyler shook his head, bemused. While they made small talk, and placed a food order, he studied the agent, still trying hard to figure him out.

As a person, Kellen presented an appealing

package, Tyler had to give him that. Kellen was of average height and build—nothing too extraordinary there. He was handsome, but that wasn't extraordinary either. What defined Kellen Rossiter was something intangible, and it radiated straight through his eyes, his carriage, and demeanor. In a word, that intangible quality had a name: magnetism.

He was easy, and friendly.

So far.

Kellen wore a gray silk suit, a crisp white dress shirt, and a deep blue tie that added a splash of color to the ensemble. Tyler would have felt a bit underdressed, since he wore simple black slacks paired with a loose fitting polo shirt, but Kellen was all about business, and since this was the start of his day, the attire was to be expected.

Tyler ticked off the seconds until he could reclaim his peace of mind, and enjoy spending more of his time with Amy. Once this breakfast and the meeting to follow was concluded he'd rest a lot easier. First things first, though; he needed to give Kellen Rossiter his full attention, and do so with an open heart, and mind.

About mid-way through a delicious and hearty meal—during which Kellen's recommendations were accepted and enjoyed—the hostess checked in at their table. "How is everything, Mr. Rossiter?"

"Very good, as always. Thanks."

She smiled at Tyler. "I wanted to say that I'm glad to see you here, Mr. Brock. I'm Janie Field, the hostess here, and I'm a big fan of your music. Congratulations on its success."

That took Tyler by pleasant and unexpected surprise. He gave her a friendly smile. "Thank you very much. I appreciate you saying that."

"You're welcome, and keep it up. Enjoy your meal, and if you need anything, just let us know."

Tyler watched her leave, still flushed by a thrill that never diminished when he came upon people who enjoyed, and were influenced by, his music. He gave Kellen a quick glance before digging in again. "They sure do take good care of you here, Kellen."

Kellen continued to eat, but his lips twitched, as though he could barely contain a chuckle. "Humility is such a rare treat to find in my neck of the woods, Tyler. Thanks for that. Janie came over here to meet you, not cater to me. Trust me on that."

Tyler shrugged it off. "Mm-hmm."

They finished breakfast; Kellen leaned back after sliding a credit card into the padded bill holder. "Shall we continue this at my office?"

Nerves came back with a wicked force. "Sure. Thanks for breakfast. It was great."

The bill was taken, and settled. "Glad to do it, Tyler. C'mon. We can walk from here."

❧❧

Once again, the walk helped. Motion cleared his head. By the time they reached the high-rise office building, Tyler had offered up final prayers for calm, and God's answers. By the time they walked into the elevator, and Kellen directed them to the twentieth floor, Tyler felt emotionally and physically prepared for whatever might come.

The doors opened upon an impressive suite, but he had expected no less. In Kellen's office, Tyler's gaze trailed to a pair of unframed abstract paintings that decorated the wall. He wandered across the threshold, continuing to look around. A glass-topped desk, trimmed in mahogany, was accented by a leather chair that looked plush and comfortable. The chair resided at a slight tilt before a panoramic view of downtown Nashville framed by floor-to-ceiling windows. A thick, cream area rug, bordered and slashed by deep burgundy, silenced their footfalls, and he now noticed an inlayed beverage service, bookshelves illuminated by recessed lights. A pair of leather chairs were positioned in front of the desk. Tyler sank into one, trying not to be obvious about the way he clutched the arms of the chair. Kellen sat behind his desk and thumbed fast through a small stack of messages.

OK, OK, I get the message—this is the big leagues, Tyler thought.

Kellen tossed the paper slips aside and stretched back a bit, giving Tyler a smile. "Let's get down to it, huh?"

Tyler nodded, and leaned back as well.

"Obviously I want to represent you. My idea is this: you're a phenomenal Christian artist. But the inherent problem with contemporary Christian music, as I see it, is a lack of mainstream exposure. The music's good, but the artists aren't getting the push they need to be heard by more listeners." Kellen shrugged. "Some artists, in my view, have the chops to bust through that barrier and cross over. Obviously you're here because I believe you're that caliber performer. I want your professional growth to match the potential I see in every one of your recordings."

Tyler didn't answer right away. Instead, he studied the man before him and constructed a figurative blockade against any kind of pride, or selfish pleasure that declaration might inspire. Only then did he weigh in. "Likewise I'm sure I don't need to build a ladder to the doubts I have. The doubts have nothing to do with you, per se, or your intentions, per se. I'm honestly flattered to be here. My fears come in at the exact point where I might be expected to give up parts of who and what I am in order to satisfy the 'greater PR good.'"

Kellen seemed about to speak, but Tyler continued on. "Furthermore, what about the people I work with? What about Dave, and Rebecca, and the team who've seen me through everything, right from the start? I don't want wholesale changes just because I sign on with an A-List agent."

Throughout Tyler's turn at bat, Kellen's lips tightened into a firm line. He sighed. "You're still not getting it, Tyler, and that puzzles me. I'm not about changes; I'm about enhancements to a package I already believe in wholeheartedly. I believe so much that I've already taken a bit of initiative. Let me show you something." Kellen slid open a desk drawer to his right and extracted a stapled set of papers. He held them out. "Give this a look."

Puzzled, Tyler took custody. "OK."

Kellen rose. "Can I get you some water?"

"Sure, that'd be great. Thanks."

Kellen went to the beverage service. While ice chinked into glasses and water splashed, Tyler looked at the information Kellen provided. What he found was a playlist—dated two weeks ago—for WNIC radio in Detroit. Over the span of two days, *Amazing Grace* was highlighted six times.

Tyler blinked. "You did this? You set up 'NIC to play *Amazing Grace*?"

Kellen looked over his shoulder, his gaze tagging

Tyler's. He shrugged, waiting.

"You did this, while I was back home in Detroit, performing at Woodland?"

"I thought it would be a good idea to deliver a bump to your exposure while you were home."

"But you had no right to do that! I'm not your client!"

Kellen was nonplussed by Tyler's agitated retort. "I made a phone call, that's all. Consider it a freebie. My only intent was for your song to get added airplay, and, yeah, for you to catch a glimpse of what I can do for you. If you walk away from the gesture, no harm done, but the facts remain." He gestured toward the papers. "It worked. It worked because your music is *good*, Tyler."

"Actually, I heard it when I was at my pastor's house." Tyler studied the play list again, and he couldn't quell the wash of disappointment. The exciting moment he had shared with his family and friends dimmed now, as though a slight "cheat" had taken place to give his song a push. Or had it? Was he being overly defensive with regard to a harmless, helpful act on Kellen's part? Tides were sweeping him onto a new mission field, whether he welcomed it or not. "It's just...I thought the song had received air play on its own merits."

Kellen returned from the bar service and shot him a hard look. "It did." He approached his desk carrying two crystal glasses. He handed one to Tyler and resumed his seat. "The song, the music, *the message*, it's all based on merit, and it's all *you*. I just touched base with a connection—reached out to the programming director at WNIC and put you on his radar. Tyler, that's what I *do*."

Tyler sighed, and he couldn't stifle a nervous, uncomfortable shift.

"You know, you might want to get over yourself a little bit." Kellen bit off the words. "I'm not the devil in this scenario, and if you want to know the truth, I think that's part of what's got you so riled up and unsettled right now. It's also part of why you've been avoiding me. You're running scared from opportunity."

"Nice job of salesmanship." But talk about finding himself *convicted*.

"I don't sugar coat." Kellen paused strategically. "And I didn't get where I'm at by being a pussycat." He leaned forward against the desk; his eyes went narrow. "I'm tenacious and relentless about going after whatever will serve me and my clients for the best. I'm not asking you to give up who and what you are. That'd spell disaster. I'm not asking you to spew expletives on stage in front of hundreds and thousands of zoned-out fans. That stuff turns my gut as much as it does yours."

"I don't sugar coat either, so let me be just as frank."

Kellen gestured openly and sat back in his chair. "Please. That's what today's all about."

"No matter what you want from me, expect from me, or try to accomplish with regard to my career, my symbol is a cross. It'll never be a bar chart in some media popularity poll. You'll end up asking me to compromise. You'll end up asking me to move just far enough away from a Christian message to dilute my mission. For the sake of sales and exposure. It's not worth it."

"Wrong. I'm asking you to loosen the reins just enough to reach more people. People who need what you offer. I want to help you spread your message on a larger stage. Isn't that why you perform? Isn't that why you've created that Christian message to begin with? To reach people?"

Tyler had no ready rebuttal to that piece of analysis. Kellen nodded slowly, his eyes unflinching. "A large number of Christian artists have remained true to their message of faith and Christianity, but at the same time they moved forward into mainstream markets. I play hardball, but I have convictions, too. My convictions lead me to the belief that your time is here. You possess exactly the degree of talent, charisma, and message to swing open a powerful door. Take it to the next level, Brock. You've got the will to make that happen? You ready? If you are, I'll make it come to be."

"That's where you're wrong. *God* will make it come to be, not you." Tyler fought against two diametrically opposed forces in his nature: Ambition versus mission. Passion for music versus passion for God. He had to fight hard to make sure he remained true to himself, and his faith. "I won't move forward without God, and who and what He brings to my music. That's my final answer."

Kellen leaned back, steepling his fingertips, tapping them lightly against his lips. "I respect that. But I also believe you can do both. In fact, maybe that's why God has put me into your pathway. Think about it."

Kellen's challenge left Tyler off center. Would this extraordinary offer mean serving two masters? Dividing his heart and loyalty? In the heat of this charged, electric exchange, he didn't know the answer. He needed prayer time. *Serious* prayer time.

That, Tyler promptly recognized, was God's answer, wafting through his heart, providing that needed certainty of course.

"I'm not sure yet, Kellen. Until I am, and I'll let you know my answer either way, give me some time to think about this, and pray about it. In *peace.*"

Kellen's lips curved. Admiration shone from his jet-colored eyes. "Fair enough, Brock. Fair enough."

The man was a tiger. Tyler had to give him credit for that, and part of him recognized clearly that Kellen Rossiter would be a formidable champion—if black and white could ever be comfortably reconciled.

As those thoughts crested through Tyler's mind, Kellen ropened the desk drawer and removed a Bible. Tyler could tell instantly the item was no prop. The spine featured numerous, deep creases. The cover was worn and a bit frayed at the edges.

Kellen handed it over. "Look it over for a second," he invited quietly.

Tyler paged through the thin, onionskin pages with reverence. It was full of penned notations, highlights of verses, all of it in various shades, but all of it in one person's handwriting. On the front page, the Bible was inscribed to Kellen, from his parents, with a confirmation date inscribed just beneath.

"I'm not trying to sway you with religion," Kellen continued. "That's not how I operate. My faith isn't something I use as a bargaining chip. But in this case, I want to demonstrate commonality." He gestured toward the black-leather volume. "I can't share this with many of the people I come into contact with. It's just not built into the nature of this business. But when I come upon an artist like you, when I see your message, and recognize its impact, I get hungry. On your behalf, and on God's behalf."

Stunned, Tyler lifted his eyes briefly. Kellen regarded him in steady silence. Tyler continued to turn pages, and he ended up in Proverbs. Though he didn't really believe in playing "Bible Roulette" he didn't think and ended up at Proverbs 3:5-6 by mere happenstance:

Trust in the Lord with all your heart, and lean not on your own understanding; in all your ways acknowledge him, and he will make your paths straight.

Last night's conversation with Amy played through his mind. In regard to their relationship, in regard to Kellen Rossiter, in regard to his career, no words from God could have struck his soul with richer impact.

12

Amy came awake in slow, pleasant degrees, her body lulled by soft breezes that circled in through an open window, her mind soothed by the steady crescendo of bird-song. She stretched, issuing a quiet, happy sigh.

And then she got whapped on the forehead.

The contact came from her daughter's stray hand when a still sleeping Pyper tossed from her back to her side. Amy winced, and rubbed her head, but she squelched a pained sound because Pyper resettled instantly, softly cooing while she snuggled into the depths of her pillow. Amy re-tucked the blankets around Pyper's body, then kissed her cheek.

She rolled out of bed and prepped herself for the day as fast as she could. She was eager to find out if Tyler had returned from Nashville and what he was up to. The intimacy of sharing with one another last night had happened so naturally, with such ease. It had been perfect to while away a beautiful evening side by side with Tyler, lulled to contentment by the steady motion of a creaky porch swing, tucked together perfectly.

But she knew today's meeting with Kellen Rossiter rested heavy on his mind, and she wanted to know its outcome.

Amy's slumber had been completely serene; her world unblemished by mixed-up dreams, taut muscles and the anxieties that bore down on her day in and day out, even at rest. It was part of being a single mom, and draining though it might be, Amy wouldn't trade an instant of Pyper's life, and finding happiness for them both outside of the horrors Mark had inflicted. So, this morning she had slept in way too late. Following the call of fresh-brewed coffee, she walked down the staircase, making her way to the kitchen. The area was vacated, although a set of breakfast dishes were rinsed and stacked in the sink, most likely by RuthAnne. A flutter of disappointment moved through her at missing Tyler's aunt. Amy looked around, now noticing something that caused confusion, and then a smile. The kitchenette featured two settings of cheery, orange stoneware placed with care upon thick, dark blue placemats. Silverware and linen napkins were stationed nearby. An envelope rested atop one of the plates, bearing her name in Tyler's increasingly familiar handwriting.

She tore into it like a Christmas present.

Amy (and Pyper, too!) ~ Bacon and eggs are warm and waiting in the oven, courtesy of RuthAnne. She'll be back around 10, 10:30. She's indulging her weekly produce market fix. I'm out front when you're done, so no worries. Wake up slow, and enjoy. ~ Tyler

Amy nipped her lower lip, trying so hard to fight that lovely dissolving surrender to the belief that this could become real—and permanent—in her life.

She poured herself a mug of coffee and set it on the table. Next she found a hot pad hanging on a wall hook, and slid a serving platter full of scrambled eggs, bacon, and toast, from inside the oven. She trailed her fingertips along the arched back of the whaler's chair, lost in thought as she dished food then sat, preparing to dig in, and re-read Tyler's note, just because it made her feel…treasured.

She filled an empty and grateful tummy, with Tyler's note her accompaniment. The gesture got her to thinking. She really needed to put together something for him to commemorate his recent visit to Woodland. She should create something special, like an album of the best pictures she had taken at the concert. Or maybe something even more immediate, like—

"Mornin'!"

RuthAnne entered the kitchen through its side door, delivering a happy nod as she hefted a stash of bags onto the counter with a thud. She began to unpack groceries, and Amy stood to help. Her arrival couldn't have been more perfectly timed. It synced right up to the idea Amy had brewing.

"Good morning, RuthAnne. How was the market?"

"Excellent selections, I tell you. Sit down and finish eating! I've got this."

"I'm done. No problem." There were all kinds of fragrant, fresh vegetables, some cantaloupe, a watermelon, and a couple packs of blueberries. Amy stored what items she could, then turned to Tyler's aunt. "Hey, RuthAnne, do you happen to know what Tyler's favorite dinner is?"

RuthAnne paused and thought about it for a moment. "I make a chicken stew that he always seems to love."

"Would you mind showing me how to make it? Sometime in the next day or two I'd like to treat him to something special, if it's not a family secret or anything."

"Oh, it's no such thing. I'd be happy to share it

with you." RuthAnne continued to put away the food. "We'd need some chicken breasts—maybe we could make a run to the store and pick them up. We'd have to prep it in the morning and let it stew for the rest of the day."

"Thank you! I think that'd be wonderful."

"Y'all are off to the falls today, right?"

"Yes, we are. And I guess Tyler's out front."

RuthAnne nodded, and she grinned. "Waiting."

Lifted by the prospect, Amy retrieved her dishes from the table and gave them a rinse before setting them in the dishwasher. After that, she exited the house through the front door, and when she looked around the porch, found nothing but empty seats and extinguished hurricane lamps on wicker tables. The memory of sharing this space, the flickering candlelight, with Tyler seeped into her soul and left happiness in its wake.

Trotting down the few steps leading to the front yard, she found him, almost hidden from view as he knelt by the flowerbeds, hard at work weeding. For a few unguarded moments, Amy savored the sight. "Well if this doesn't bring back some memories."

He looked up, the late-morning sun glimmering in his dark blond hair. His skin was richly tanned, his arms sinewy and strong as he continued to yank away traces of overgrowth. He wore a pair of faded cut-offs and a white t-shirt that did odd, fluttery things to her insides. "So get on down here and help. We always made a great team."

"Glad I just ate a hearty breakfast." She shot him a teasing look, and then knelt next to him on the thick pad where he paused for a few seconds. "I loved the note, too. So far, the entire morning has me feeling quite pampered." She pulled away some scrub grass and weeds. "Well, until now, that is."

"Mission accomplished then. Until now, that is."

They worked at weeding for a bit, but then Amy couldn't wait any longer. Curiosity was eating her alive. "So…how'd it go?"

Tyler shook his head, but didn't miss a beat in his landscaping detail. "I'm working myself senseless— after a sleepless night, and following a very intense meeting—because it fills me with equal parts fear and thrill to realize I'm just about ready to sign on with him."

Wow. Amy settled back on her haunches, ignoring the overgrowth for a minute. "Really."

"Really."

"So you're ready to make the decision, but you're not completely content."

"Truth to tell, I probably won't be content until we strike an agreement and start to actually move forward. Part of me is blown away by him; he's a really impressive guy. And, in basic terms, I trust his intent. But there's this other part of me that's scared of the whole rug-being-ripped-out-from-under-me thing."

She looked into Tyler's eyes. A world of long-standing friendship and knowing, was revealed in their depths.

"That's why we pray." They spoke the words in a perfect unison that left Amy wistful for the ease of their youth.

Tyler touched her cheek with the tip of a clean finger. "God truly knows how much I miss those youth group days when we'd gather in a circle, talk about our troubles just like we are right now, and end on that very claim."

"I feel the same way. It was so simple then."

"To a degree." A pause followed, ripe with an underscore of tender emotion. "Where's Pyper?"

Amy chuckled. "Still sleeping. Hey, do I have a bruise on my forehead?"

Tyler studied her. "No. Why?"

"Good. I was worried there for a second. She walloped me a good one just before I got out of bed."

"Restless sleeper?"

"Yeah. Always has been."

Tyler shook his head and his wry grin had her curious.

"What's that look all about?"

"You. You're the opposite of a restless sleeper. I remember the trip home from Pennsylvania. You executed a none-too-subtle seating arrangement that put me between you and Carlie. Remember?"

Amy pulled dandelions and more overgrowth from the soil around the bushes. "She wanted to sit by you. I was being a good and gracious friend."

"But I was caught in the middle. You fell asleep on my shoulder about a half hour after we started home. My arm went to sleep and my whole right side basically went stiff because I didn't want to move. You snuggled in like a cat takin' a nap."

A delicious sensation of weakness seeped through Amy's insides. "I don't even remember that."

"Well, honey, you were asleep at the time."

Tyler's expression made Amy laugh though she felt suddenly shy. Infinitely warm.

"Frankly, I would have taken a lightning bolt before I moved and disturbed you and made you move away. I loved it."

Amy picked up their refuse piles and stuffed them

into a nearby recycle bag. That was the thing about Tyler. He'd never, ever, take a loved one for granted, or fail to see to their comfort. "I swear, Tyler, I didn't deserve you then, and I question why you think I deserve you now." Awash in high emotion, in dreams of all that could have been, Amy leaned in and kissed his cheek, wishing for so much more from this man. "I sure am glad to be with you, though. Truly."

He turned, and his gaze roved over her like a slow-moving caress. "Ditto."

"Mommy? Wh're you?"

The summons jarred them apart just when Amy had hoped for a bit more—like that kiss she had been aching for. Through the open front door, she saw Pyper slow-step down the stairway, holding tight to the built-in banister. Pyper rubbed her eyes and yawned big.

"I'm right here, snug-a-bug. C'mon out to the porch."

"Mm'kay."

Tyler watched Pyper's progress and grinned. "She's got every one of your cutest mannerisms, Amy."

"Mm-hmm. Including a wicked right hook."

"I'll keep that in mind. Morning, Pyper," Tyler called out. "You ready to go for a hike, and see a big, beautiful waterfall?"

"Mm-hmm. Hi, Tyler." She pushed open the screen door and padded across the porch in her bare feet. A long, cotton nightgown rippled around her ankles in the breeze. Her hair was an adorable, uncombed tangle; her eyes sleep coated, but slowly coming alive.

"Did you sleep well?" he asked.

"Mm-hmm. I'm hungry." Right on cue, probably

hearing their voices, out came RuthAnne with the place setting full of food that had been saved for Pyper. A tumbler of milk completed the meal. "Thank you, Ruthie." Pyper dazzled RuthAnne with a smile, then looked at Amy. "Las' night, when we said g'night, she said I could call her Ruthie."

The adults exchanged smiles, and Pyper sat down on one of the big, padded wicker chairs; setting her plate on the table in front of it, she dug in.

"Mommy, can I help with my diggin' tools Tyler got me?" She asked the question while munching a mouth full of toast and bacon.

"Tell you what. Your mama and I are gonna call it quits on the gardening for now, so we can all go have fun. Wanna give me some help tomorrow morning?"

Pyper downed some milk that left a white mustache on her upper lip. "Mm-hmm. I want to."

"Great. I appreciate that." Tyler stretched his back, then stood and trotted up the stairs. "I'm gonna change real quick, then we can head out. I want to show you some of the places I love here in Tennessee."

Pyper didn't say anything when he passed, but she watched him with careful intensity. When he was gone, Pyper returned to her breakfast. "He's bein' real fun, Mommy. Like when we were at home."

The words were kind, the tone, though, was just this side of doubtful. Amy figured it out. Pyper was waiting for Tyler to betray that fledgling bit of trust and growing connection. How could that be helped, after all? How could Pyper continue to refuse such a consistent, tenderhearted man?

Again, an answer came to Amy, whispering through her soul like an answer from God. *Time. Give it time.*

꙰

"Do you like waterfalls, Pyper?" Tyler asked. They were just over an hour outside of Franklin, the top down on his Mustang, the warm air, blue sky, and sunshine filling Amy's senses.

"I never saw one up close before." From her spot in the back seat, Pyper watched the world zip by. Amy noticed the way her daughter took everything in: the hills, the horses, the farms and homes, the cows that made her exclaim and giggle.

Tyler turned off a hilly, two-lane highway that snaked through an unspoiled, quiet area. He parked in front of a simple metal barricade, next to a hand-lettered sign that read: *Rutledge Falls*. "Well, let's take care of that right now. Follow me, ladies."

The tumble and crash of water echoed around them as they scrabbled down a narrow gravel and grass pathway. They clung to sturdy tree trunks and stepped carefully over the stones and bramble that covered the uneven terrain. After descending as far as they could, Pyper stopped in her tracks and tugged hard on Amy's hand. "Mommy! Look at it! Look at it!"

Their hike ended at a stunning view of a four-tiered, sixty-foot cascade of mountain water that sang through the air like ancient music. The sparkling flow tumbled and sprayed into a wide pool far below that rippled with life. Tyler held Amy's other hand; the three-way connection left her elated as they stood on a wide rock ledge, watching the never-ending cascade. "I know! Isn't it gorgeous?"

"I remember once, a few years ago, they filmed a movie out here," Tyler informed. "There were film crews swarming this place just like the ants on that ant hill over there." He pointed at a nearby mound of earth teeming with insects and Pyper propped her hands on her knees, bending promptly to investigate.

Tyler continued. "I remember watching the movie afterwards. The scene they filmed here was all about this group of kids having a fun day in the summertime, diving into that pool of water down there by swinging on ropes, and—"

"Oh, now you've done it," Amy muttered in a teasing way, already knowing what was coming as the result of Tyler's added detail about Rutledge Falls.

First came a squeal that launched a family of birds from a nearby tree with flapping wing noise and irritated squawks. "I wanna rope swing! I wanna rope swing! Where are they? Can I go? Can I swing? Mommy, did we bring my floaty vest?"

Amy laughed. "Way to step into that one, Tyler."

Pyper bounced around, searching desperately for a rope swing, and the means by which to get to the base of the waterfall far below. "I had no idea," he muttered back. Tyler blinked hard, and then addressed Pyper. "There's no rope to swing on, sugar beet. Sorry. They only did that for the movie, with cranes and hoists and stuff. To be honest, it's a tough proposition for even trained hikers to get to the bottom."

Pyper frowned, but wandered to the edge of the outcropping, looking down at the bubbling, gurgling water. Wearing a slight frown, she studied the waterfall, then its emerald colored reservoir, with longing. "What a bummer."

Tyler gave Amy a sardonic look. "See what Hollywood does? Builds things up and then dashes 'em against stones."

Amy giggled at that verdict.

He refocused on Pyper. "The next place we're going to, Fall Creek Falls, has a beautiful waterfall, too, and that one we can actually see from the bottom."

Appeased, Pyper's excitement returned. "Cool!"

"Nice save." Amy whispered the compliment, more than happy to keep her hand snug in his.

"I'm learning on the fly."

∂∽∾

Fall Creek Falls was everything Tyler promised: lush, unspoiled and radiant with life. When they reached the base of the falls, Amy edged her rucksack off her shoulder and unzipped it in a hurry, not wanting the inspiration or the play of light and color to escape her. She lifted out her camera and slid the strap into place, beginning to chronicle the nature display. Water burst, tumbled and spilled. The sweet aroma of brightly colored flowers combined pleasingly with the heavier musk of damp earth. Rocks, sun, and field unified into a view that left her breathless. Crouching, she framed a gorgeous shot of Pyper, who stood in ankle-deep grass surrounded by a sea of bell-shaped purple flowers that were nestled into the body of thick, green leaves. Water glistened and flashed, the spray shooting off rainbows as it tumbled over gleaming black ledges of Chattanooga shale.

In sun-drenched profile, Pyper's hair tossed softly in the wind, her eyes cast upward in wonder as she studied the waterfall. The sky was a perfect, stark blue above her; thick, leaf-laden tree branches textured the shot.

Amy clicked away, losing herself, moving from

spot to spot to capture moments, freeze memories and images into a place she could revisit over and over again. Creating shot after shot, she couldn't stop smiling. Photography was such a joy. Photography filled a calling in her soul and lifted her up.

The meadow was a riot of colorful wildflowers and Pyper set about playing in the middle of it all. Amy crouched low once more, framing. Not satisfied, she laid flat on her stomach, capturing images of her daughter as Pyper stripped off her sandals and dipped her feet in the pool of water that crested nearby. Then, Amy laid on her back and lifted up just a bit, executing a shot of Tyler, who stood not far away, enjoying Pyper's playful antics as well. His tall, lean frame blocked the sun from invading the picture. The overall effect was like rays of light bursting to life all around his darkened silhouette.

She lowered her camera slowly, consumed by him. Suddenly, all she could think about was capturing him somehow; she wanted to retain the perfect beauty of this time together to help comfort her in the empty days to come. Without him. After all, this idyllic week would have to come to an end...and that thought caused her throat to swell tight with a sharp stab of pain.

Tyler squatted, taking in their surroundings with a contented expression. He brushed his open hand against the carpet of purple flowers. She couldn't quell her response to the image; she lifted the camera and reeled off a few more pictures. He turned his head, to look at her, and his quirk of a smile left her aching to capture it forever. She fought against being so blatant about photographing him, but in the end, she couldn't resist. The shots came to life in digital form, touching her heart as surely as the touch of his hand in hers.

Tyler joined her, offering up a trio of the tiny purple flowers she had been admiring. "You seem to be in your element."

Amy accepted them happily, and tilted her head to look into his eyes. "Thanks for these. And, believe me, I'm thinking the same thing."

"Good." The emphasis he placed on that word made heat flow to her cheeks in a subtle reaction of pleasure. His focus remained relentless, intent, and compelling. Amy sniffed at the blooms, enjoying the sweet, delicate perfume. "They're Virginia bluebells."

"They're gorgeous." In secret, Amy tingled, already planning to add these tiny flowers to the hyacinths he had given her back in Michigan, the ones which were now pressed carefully into the pages of her Pennsylvania mission photo album.

"Now, I want you to do me a favor."

"OK."

Tyler slid a fingertip beneath the thick strap of the camera. He lifted it up and over Amy's head, taking possession. "Look at everything again. Take it in. Only, this time, without the filter, without the buffer of a lens. With nothing but the gratitude and joy I've seen in your eyes all morning. Take it in, Amy. It's God's gift."

Dumfounded, she considered his request, and then, she obeyed. Propping back on her hands, she settled comfortably. Utterly at rest, Amy took in the scent of damp earth, the rough texture of twigs contrasted against the softness of the green leaves of ground cover that pressed against her palm. The petals and deep green leaves burst into life all around. Water crashed. Birds cawed. Subtle moisture, an after-spray from the waterfall, touched her cheeks, her neck, and arms left bare by a sleeveless blouse. Still, Amy couldn't help but think of her surroundings in terms of pictures, framing shot after gorgeous shot in her mind. Memories. Each image was a memory she didn't want to lose to the elusive, swirling fog of time. And distance.

Nevertheless, a thrill of delight worked through her. Pure happiness took over with as much power as the waterfall that formed a down rush just a few yards away. Tyler was right. This was truly God's gift.

So, she revealed herself in response to the exercise he imposed. "It's not that I don't *see* my world, or appreciate it when I'm taking pictures."

Seated next to her, Tyler pulled up a leg and crooked an arm around it. He nodded in agreement, waiting on more.

"Maybe it's protective—a bit of a hiding place—but overall, it's just that pictures are precious to me. They forever capture a moment that can never, ever be replicated. They're tangible pieces of the lives we've lived."

A life Mark had destroyed with a sledgehammer. Amy refused to dwell on that fact for long, though. After all, she had Pyper. Always, always her beloved daughter.

Amy closed her eyes, face lifted to the sun. "I know it sounds selfish and even a bit simplistic, and maybe it's not even a good way of coping, but something about my photography helps me grasp anew the fact that I won't ever be left that desolate again, that abandoned."

"Perfectly natural, human reaction. Just remember one very vital component to those emotions you're feeling."

"What's that?"

"You've never, ever been abandoned. Not by God most especially, and not by the friends and family God placed in your pathway—and Pyper's."

Amy heard the familiar sound of shutter clicks, and the subtle crunch of Tyler's feet as he moved quietly around her, taking pictures. Amy's revelry ended. She looked up at him with a smile not meant for the camera, or pictures, but instead reflecting sheer gratitude for the words he had spoken.

"Hey, Pyper," Tyler called, "c'mere to your mama."

Pyper nodded and ran to where Amy sat. Spontaneously she threw her arms around Amy's neck. Cheek to cheek they looked at Tyler with wide happy smiles as he clicked his own series of shots.

But Amy knew the picture she wanted the most, and she was determined not to let the moment pass without the acknowledgment of something precious and special that she wanted to be able to call upon forevermore. "Wait. I've got a timer setting, and a mini tripod. Let's do a shot of the three of us."

Amy set up the camera on a nearby tree stump and she blocked out a fun shot of the three of them laying on their stomachs, looking up at the camera. They lined up—Tyler, then Amy, then Pyper with their chins propped on their hands. The timer counted down, and Tyler's words came back to her, hugely magnified by the wants of her heart:

You've never, ever been abandoned. Not by God most especially, and not by the friends and family God placed in your pathway—and Pyper's.

The truth of that statement resounded through her

spirit for long hours after their return home from Fall Creek Falls.

13

Tyler kept Pyper in his peripheral vision while he worked in the yard. She played with the bag of gardening toys he'd picked up for her last week at a local dime store—for all of fifteen minutes. Then, she'd returned to the house and came back to their spot in the yard, carrying the sparkly kickball he had also acquired for her visit.

At present, she blasted the ball through the yard, chased it, then let loose with follow-up kicks, and giggles. Amy was out grocery shopping with RuthAnne, and so far, Pyper had seemed pretty comfortable to be left alone with him. It helped, though, that Amy promised to be gone only for a short time—a half hour to forty-five minutes at the most. It also helped that Pyper had something to do, outside, in wide-open spaces.

Tyler's bit of yard maintenance was nearly finished, and he loved the results. Yeah, the work was a pain, but no arguing with the polished up results. Pyper went on a mad dash again and Tyler watched, enjoying her increased abandon and childish delight.

He started to dispose of the weeds; that's when Pyper jerked violently in mid-stride to chase the ball. Then, she went perfectly still. She didn't shout; she didn't make a sound. She tumbled to a sitting position, drew up her legs tight and began to rock back and forth. Her eyes sparkled with moisture. Tyler stopped what he was doing, watching as she trembled and rubbed her left leg, her eyes wide with shock, and what he could only assume was some form of pain.

"Sugar beet? You OK?" He started toward her, but she winced away from his approach. Tyler froze. He knelt to her level, soft grass cushioning his knees. He was puzzled, but game to try reaching out to her. "What happened, honey?"

Her eyes brimmed. Tears trickled over, and her chin quaked. She didn't look at him. Instead, she stared at her leg where he noticed an angry, blooming welt of red. "I won't cry." The trembles increased. "I promise. I won't. I'll be very, very quiet." She whispered the mantra to herself, not Tyler, still clutching at her leg, curling in on herself.

The poor thing had been stung on the leg by a bee, and she trembled more from fear than pain, backing away from him in meek retreat. Tyler didn't need extra reasons to detest the emotional havoc Mark Samuels had wreaked, but this one skyrocketed to the top of his list.

"Pyper, can you let me help?"

"No. S'okay. I'm fine."

Once more, the words were a whisper. She was leagues away from fine, and he knew it. She remained tightly crouched, the angry-looking bite her only focus. Soft hiccups and choked sobs accompanied Pyper's now rolling tears.

Tyler remained squatted and steady, respecting her appointed measure of distance. Likely the freshly injected venom sang hot through her calf. He tried once more. "I can help, Pyper. I can make the pain go away. Please trust me. I'd be happy to help take care of you."

She looked up at him hesitantly, through glittering, watery eyes. "Mommy's not here, an' it really, really hurts. I'll be good if you help me, Tyler. I promise I will. You won't have to be mad at me like Daddy. I won't cry or make sad noises." She eyed the bee sting and rocked back and forth. "I'll be very, very quiet," she whispered.

Rage simmered deep in his blood, rage toward a man he'd gladly throttle—but he knew that reaction was instinctive, rather than Christian. Pyper was the only one who mattered right now, and Tyler determined to use this episode to show Pyper a different pattern of male behavior.

He moved closer, taking his time. "Did you get stung by a bee?" he asked gently.

Pyper dissolved. She nodded emphatically, reached up for him and held on tight, sobbing against him. "I got stunged!"

"Honey, I'm so sorry. I've been stung many times before, and it hurts so bad. I understand just how you feel. You don't have to hold back around me. I don't mind tears, and I don't mind sad noises. Honest."

For a long, soothing moment, he just held her tight, right there in the cool, damp grass, cradling her close, rocking just a bit. Pyper rested, content and at ease, relaxing in steady increments. Once she calmed, he took her hand in his and helped her to stand.

"Come on, Pyper. I've got a lotion that will cool the pain away, and we can get the stinger out. Once we do you'll feel lots better."

Despite wobbly legs, she followed him, keeping her hand tucked in his. She looked up at him with a mix of expectation, hope, and uncertainty. *Lord*, he petitioned with urgency, *let me handle this right. Help me assure this precious little girl, and help me show her Your loving care.*

"Let's go to the bathroom." He directed her inside. "I've got cotton balls and calamine lotion that'll fix you up just fine."

Pyper nodded. She sat on the commode and after retrieving a few necessities from the medicine cabinet, Tyler knelt in front of her, lifting her leg by the calf. "You're one brave young lady." He pushed up the hem of her Capri-style jeans. She went taut watching him uncap the calamine lotion and tip the bottle until a dab of it colored the cotton ball. He stopped, and looked deliberately into her wide, scared eyes. "It's going to feel cold. That's all."

She rolled her lips in and winced as he applied the medication, but then she relaxed, and stared at her leg in wonder. "It's sorta like a ice cube. It's workin' I think."

The harder part was coming. "I need to try to get the stinger out. While I do that, know what we can do?"

"What?"

"Sing a song. What's your favorite?"

She shrugged. Her hair tossed against her shoulders with the motion. "What do you like to sing when you're scared?" Her question was spoken in a tentative voice, as though she didn't want to be irritating, or weak. *God*, he prayed, *this little girl is such an angel.*

While they talked, and decided to sing their A-B-C's, Tyler kept her attention away from the fact that he squeezed the red welt; that he gently worked at the tip of the stinger's exposed end until it slid free. She flinched at one point, when he had to squeeze her skin pretty tight, but at least he didn't end up needing to use tweezers. Just seeing the instrument might have terrified her. He applied another dab of calamine to the wound, wanting to soothe and heal anything he had freshly exposed. A Band-aid later, she was ready for action once again.

"I wanna see it," Pyper said, taking him by complete surprise.

"See what, sugar beet?"

"The stinger thingy."

He had set it on the sink for the time being, intending to wipe things down and toss it into the trash once Pyper was taken care of. He gave her a grin, because she looked a whole lot braver and happy now that they had achieved crisis containment. "Really? You do?"

"Mm-hmm."

Tyler slid the miniscule black stinger into the palm of his hand and held it out for her inspection. In fact, they both bent over it. Tyler imagined they looked like a pair of scientists on the brink of some world-altering discovery.

"Sheesh," she muttered.

"Sheesh what?"

"Sheesh that stupid tiny thing hurt me. How'd it *do* that?"

They left the bathroom behind, and Tyler launched into a child-friendly dissertation on bee stings and venom. Without any encouragement on Tyler's part, Pyper slipped her hand into his and looked up at him with a beauteous smile.

Music played through his heart with a joy that was absolute. That's probably what inspired another idea.

"Know what I want to do now?"

"What's that, Tyler?" She was openly and completely adoring now. Tyler wanted to rejoice— laugh, shout and dance.

"I want to teach you the most fun song ever to be played on the piano."

"Really?" Her steps stalled. Her eyes went big, like clear blue saucers. "You'd let me actually play your piano? Touch the keys 'n stuff? I'd be so, so careful!"

"Sure I would. Piano's need to be respected, but they need to be played, too. After all, that's the only way they make music."

"An'…an' you'd let me?" Her hero worship was now blatant.

"Come on over here, sugar beet. I'm gonna teach you how to play Chopsticks."

"I love that song!"

Happy moments passed—with plunked piano keys, laughter and the two of them cuddled side by side on the bench of Tyler's piano. She was pretty good, too, at catching on to rhythms and melodies. Focused and determined, this bright little girl picked up on Tyler's instructions with ease.

Soon enough, activity in the entryway of the great room caught Tyler's attention. That's when he saw Amy come through the door, grocery sacks in tow, watching the vignette from a spot just to their right. RuthAnne followed close behind. Amy stood there for a moment, cataloguing the scene, and the look on her face touched Tyler's heart. Surprise, disbelief, love—for Pyper, and for him—it was all right there in her cobalt eyes.

"Hey, baby," she addressed Pyper, setting the sacks on the floor at her feet. "You enjoying a piano lesson from Tyler?"

Music forgotten, Pyper charged into her mother's waiting arms. "I got stunged, Mommy!" She backed away just far enough to hold out her leg and point at the bandage. "An' he had to give me special lotion, and we looked at the stinger, and we sang, and then he taught me piano music. Chopsticks. He says it's the best song ever for the piano, and I think he's totally, totally right."

Not once did Tyler relinquish his visual hold on Amy. RuthAnne moved past, off to the kitchen with her own stash of food, but Amy riveted him. "I treated it with some calamine to take away the sting. It's a little swollen, but I don't think she's allergic or anything. She's been a champ. I'm real proud of her."

Pyper just glowed, her smile bouncing from him, to Amy, as she swayed happily from side to side.

Amy remained still, looking at Tyler. RuthAnne, seeming to realize the groceries Amy carried in weren't about to walk into the kitchen by themselves, lifted them up and slipped quietly away once more. Tyler noticed all this on one level, but on another, he couldn't help but wonder about one very important thing. He wished he knew what Amy was thinking. And he could only pray it was something positive, because at the moment, she looked shell-shocked.

రావ్

Tyler kept his thoughts to himself until later. That evening, he peeked through the front screen door and discovered Amy relaxing on the porch, swinging gently in her favorite seat as night rode in. A night filled by the sparkling dance of fireflies.

He left his warmly lit home behind, taking quiet steps onto the porch just in time to watch Amy stretch her arms over her head, pulling her body into a long, languorous line. She crossed her ankles as she leaned back against the plush cushions of the swing once more and issued a happy sigh. She, too, watched the lighting bug display. The insects floated throughout the yard, sparking and fading, sparking and fading.

Tyler settled next to her carefully, not wanting to disturb her, yet at the same time wanting to be close. "You seem rested. Relaxed."

Amy looked at him with a soft curve to her lips that swept against his senses. "I have to tell you, I haven't felt this good in over a year. I feel..." she stumbled over word choices. "I feel..." She came up dry again.

"Safe?"

"Yeah. That's part of it."

"Content?"

Her skin went flush with a rise in color he detected even under the bath of yellow-gold light from the hanging light above them. "You could say that, too."

He chuckled lightly and settled his arm along the back of the swing. Nudging the wooden floorboards at his feet, Tyler set the swing into motion.

"It's just that, my life is kind of a sun up 'til sundown marathon session. Being able to rest feels really good."

He watched her intently, prompting her without words.

"I'm not complaining. Not in the least. If I didn't have the marathon session, I wouldn't have Pyp. She gives me so much joy that I couldn't, and wouldn't, trade a single teardrop or a single exhausted moment with her."

Amy closed her eyes and breathed in deep. The rise and fall of her chest told him clearly that she soaked up this moment and captured it in her system. He longed for that for her. He wanted God's love, and peace to flow and soothe— thereby healing an ages-old wound.

But Tyler didn't press; he was content to let her rest, and savor the silence. He knew her well enough— and trusted the strength of their relationship enough— to allow her to unwind and reveal herself at her own pace.

For the time being, Tyler tipped his head back and relaxed into the evening as well, smiling to himself as the realization occurred that she wasn't the only one basking in contentment right now.

The screen door squeaked and banged. Small, fast-moving feet padded across the porch, disappearing into the soft grass just beyond the porch. Next to him, Amy chuckled. She didn't even open her eyes. "This has got to be a small taste of heaven."

Tyler rejoiced in the way she simply surrendered herself, and her daughter, to a gorgeous spring night in the south.

"Mommy! Mommy, look!" Pyper's none-too-subtle summons jarred Amy to attention, but she smiled at the reason for the interruption.

Tyler followed her line of sight. Pyper had spotted the darting, flashing fireflies.

Excitement gone, Pyper suddenly went unnaturally still. She turned toward them fast, brows knit tight. Her alarm was plain to see, despite the lengthening shadows and the encroaching darkness of night. "Are they good bugs or bad bugs?"

"Those are good bugs, Pyper. They're fireflies, and they won't sting you," Tyler reassured her. Down here, we call 'em lightning bugs, too. They just light up, and float around and play. In fact, they're a lot like *you*, sugar beet."

Relaxed now, Pyper giggled. She held her arms wide, playing and dashing, trying to touch the insects. Framed in the rippling grass of the dusk-shadowed yard; her face shone as brightly as the bevy of lighting bugs that floated through the air all around her.

"I've got a mason jar or two." Tyler made ready to stand. "Want to catch yourself a couple of 'em?"

Pyper stopped on a dime. "Oh, no, Tyler. *No.*" She shook her head, blonde curls shaking and bouncing.

The answer took Tyler by surprise. "Why's that?"

"'Cause then they wouldn't be happy anymore." Her face was so sad. So empathetic. "I just want to watch them. Right here." For emphasis she pointed at the yard in a gesture of hard punctuation. "This is where they belong. They're so pretty! I love them!"

"Know what? You're absolutely right." Tyler leaned close, curved his arm around Amy's shoulders. "Do you have *any* idea at all what a wonderful child you've raised?"

Following a lengthy look into his eyes—one he took in with deliberate, steady calm— Amy was the one who toed the floorboards to initiate a gentle swinging motion. Tyler enjoyed the gentle sway, the comfortable squeak of the chunky metal chains.

"Thanks. She owns my heart." Her voice was husky. "We're a team—it's me and her taking on the world, that's for sure." She took a breath and turned toward him. "And thanks for the way you stepped in and helped Pyper this morning. That *episode* was tough on her, in a number of ways. You scored a big round of points in the trust department, and that means the world to me."

"She was scared to death." And so different from Pyper in the here and now. Presently she squealed with delight and raced across the grounds, oblivious to everything but innocence and the joy to be found in nature.

"More of how you might react than the bee sting."

"I could tell." That statement left them at a small impasse before Tyler moved forward. "It shook you up, too. Beyond her getting stung."

"Yeah, it did." She closed her eyes; tipped her head back. Her rough tone belied the depth of her feelings. "I wish I could play you a movie from the day I left Mark. I keep thinking about it." She spoke quietly — resigned, it seemed. "I want to explain; I want you to know. It's just not an easy thing to verbalize."

Pyper trooped up the stairs, breathing heavy. She flounced into place on the swing — right between them. "I'm gettin' tired."

"You want to go inside?" Amy asked.

Pyper shrugged. "Ruthie is watchin' TV, I think. I hear her favorite game show." Pyper's eyes lit up. "She's teaching me how to crochet!" She launched from the swing. "I'm gonna go in and practice. See ya'!"

In a blaze of motion punctuated by bouncing blonde curls, Pyper pulled open the screen door and ran inside.

For a moment, Tyler went with the silence. After a while, though, he resumed their conversation, unable to fathom the nightmare Amy, and Pyper, had lived through. "I'm gonna be real direct right now." He waited, searching her face until he was sure he had her acceptance.

Amy nodded hesitantly.

He reached down just far enough to stroke her shoulder, lightly, repeatedly. "What did he do to you? Don't sugar coat it. Don't hide from it, or push it aside. I want to know you again, Amy. All of you. The good stuff and the bad."

Words didn't come; instead, she bowed her head. Her shoulders shook, and it took mere seconds for him to realize she was crying. Breaking down, in fact. Tyler gave her space to shatter, and absorb the unspoken support of his touch, while she reassembled. She drew up her knees and tucked against the side of the swing—like she had the other night. She wiped her cheeks with her hands. Her hair slid against the back of his hand, silky and soft. Lavender scent, the last traces of her perfume, lifted to him.

Instinctively he longed to ease her reaction by offering comfort. But he didn't. Something told him she needed this, desperately.

"Today brought everything back," she said, her voice shaky, her eyes distanced by memories. "It was sunny, and humid and hot. And I carried groceries." She didn't look at him. Instead, she rested her cheek on her knees and stared out at the yard and the sky. Tears glittered, rolling occasionally against her hand, and knees, but she swiped at them. "I came home from the store and he was there. Drunk out of his mind and a bottle of whiskey left open in our living room right next to the ice-filled tumbler he was using. Nice, huh?"

Tyler braced himself. "Where was Pyper?"

"In her room. Being punished by Mark for some random, meaningless reason so she'd be out of his way. She was trapped and terrified in a stuffy, hot bedroom so he could drink, and let his temper build. He had just lost his job so he was in a bad place to begin with, but I reached my breaking point. I just didn't care anymore. I fought against him in ways I never had before. It was like a reflex. Instinct."

He kept his touch rhythmic, his presence steady and open. On the inside, however, he absolutely raged.

"That day, he turned the full brunt of his fury on me. For the first time ever, I shoved right back. Oh, he'd always demean me, and make me feel worthless, but this time, it was physical, and horrible beyond anything I had ever gone through before. He shoved me, he destroyed our kitchen; he shattered a camera he knew I needed for a freelance photography job that weekend. I had dumped out his whiskey. I threw the tumbler in the sink so hard it shattered. That's when he struck me across the face. A blinding backhand. He shoved me again, this time against the edge of a counter so hard I saw stars. He was big, and strong, and he pushed me around like a rag doll when I said I was leaving."

"But Amy, thank God you did. You obviously weren't safe around him any longer."

"True." She drew in a deep breath. "But you see, the leaving was fine by him. The day I left, all he cared about was keeping me away from Pyper. Because he could. Because he knew I was out of my mind with worry and fear for her. Because he was stronger. At one point, he deliberately blocked me from Pyper's room. When he was finished toying with me, he just pushed me out the front door of our home and dead-bolted it."

Without a thing to her name. Tyler's stomach

clenched. He was sickened, but for the sake of Amy's chance at openness and healing, he swallowed back the bile. "You got her, though. How?"

Only then did she turn her head to look at him. She sniffled and blinked tiredly. "I pulled her out of her bedroom window after I tore the screen away."

The queasiness threatened to overwhelm.

She moistened her lips, and she sighed. "I left Pyper alone with him too often, and that was wrong. I see that now. But, I was so eager to embrace anything, like my freelance work, that would keep me away from him. He married me out of pity because I was pregnant, and at first he was tolerant. But after a while, even that token piece of emotion vanished. Bitterness grew, and instead of love, a sense of injustice filled him up."

She began to cry again; for the second time, Tyler didn't halt the flow. He wanted her to let go of a gut-wrenching past.

"Mark never looked at Pyper and saw our gorgeous, precocious little girl. Instead, he saw obligation and an unwanted commitment that came along way too soon in his picture-perfect life. Our marriage and Pyper's arrival crimped his ambitions, and his dreams, without any kind of warning."

"Making love is a warning, Amy. He can't plead ignorance on that count."

"And neither can I."

Tyler had to cede the point, much as it tore him up inside to think of her with anyone else but him. Still, he hadn't meant for the statement to hurt her.

"That's why I stayed with him for so long. I was in it right along with him, but I believed everything would work out. That happiness would happen."

"Amy." He spoke her name like a command. As intended, the tone re-centered her focus. "The big difference here—and I hope you listen to me carefully when I say this—is that no matter what the circumstance, you honored your marriage as best you could, and while he neglected Pyper, you never, ever did. Don't buy into the whole he-got-mad-at-me-for-getting-pregnant argument. It doesn't wash, honey. If he realized what he had, if he took care of the treasures he was given—namely you and Pyper—there's no way on earth he could be so filled with anger and bitterness, unplanned pregnancy or not."

Her gaze trained on his. "I feel like a failure, Tyler. I failed at the most important relationship we're called to create."

"Are you taking responsibility for what Mark did to you? And to Pyper? Because if you are, you need to adjust your thinking. Seriously."

Her lips curved; she gave him a wry look. "That's almost exactly what Kiara said to me before I left." She shrugged, and blew out a puff of air. "The statement rings with truth, but somehow, no matter how hard I try, it refuses to sink into my mind, and my heart."

He couldn't stand being distant from her any longer. Tyler slid his arm against her shoulders and drew her to his side, nuzzling her hair, savoring its silky texture against his cheek, and lips. "Keep trying. Like everyone else, you're a beautiful work in progress."

"I *wanted* it to work. It was *supposed* to work. It *should* have worked. What does it say to my level of commitment that I walked away?"

"That you had to maintain your welfare, and that of your daughter."

"To a degree, sure. But, how could I ever expect a man to have faith in me, and believe in my Christian convictions? Could you ever trust me, Tyler? *Really* trust me?"

He paused, and looked her straight in the eyes. "I already do."

Amy cleared her throat and shifted, relaxing against him completely. The feel of her body next to his became the completion of a season in his life that would forever revolve around Amy Maxwell. Darkness deepened, drawing in around them like a cocoon, seeping into the atmosphere with a sense of velvet intimacy. Tyler stretched his legs, nudging the swing again to maintain their motion.

Amy took in a deep, stilling breath. "You know what I keep thinking, ever since the concert? I keep thinking about how much I wish I had made different choices; that I had been smart enough to realize your worth instead of focusing on Mark with all the narrow-eyed, single-mindedness I possessed back then. Now I feel broken. I feel like such a failure...not just for the divorce, but for not seeing people as they really are. I relied on my own perceptions, and images. That was *such* a huge mistake. You and Mark are a perfect case in point. Look at what I could have had with you."

With that, the words were finally out in the open, heartbreaking, but a fissured pathway to everything that might be re-found. The words provided hope, in a chipped, but sturdy bottle. Tyler reached for her hand and held it tight. "I have a better idea. Don't look at what you could have had. Look at where you're at now. Let's look at the chance we're being given. After all, that's the whole reason I asked you to come here. And keep something else in mind."

She searched his eyes. "What's that?"

He thought about Pyper, and the breakthroughs he had made with Amy's daughter today. "Sometimes it takes the pain of a bee sting to bring about a world full of change, and a heart that's finally ready for happiness."

14

Slowly, Amy climbed the stairs to her bedroom; Pyper had just disappeared into the bathroom to change into her pajamas and brush her teeth. Amy's mind still spun at Tyler's words. All day he had laid out tantalizing breadcrumbs of come-toward-me emotions she found impossible to refuse. Since high school, his heart had belonged to her alone. Over the span of five long years apart, his feelings remained steadfast and true. Meanwhile, Amy's had taken time to emerge. It was a tentative process, but no less definite.

Sometimes it takes the pain of a bee sting to bring about a heart ready for happiness.

Do you have any idea at all what a wonderful child you've raised?

Tyler's words soaked into her soul and found rich, nourishing soil. Under his influence, her heart moved dangerously close to a complete meltdown. She gave over to him—unable to help it—and furthermore, she didn't even want to stem the tide.

A heavy gust of wind whistled through the window, billowing the curtains, smelling vaguely of rain. Amy turned, glancing outside. A late-night thunderstorm had been forecast, but up to now, the weather had held. A rumble of thunder sounded in the distance.

Amy waited for her turn in the bathroom, pulling out lightweight fleece pajamas and preparing supplies. Her mind refused to rest as she hunted for a hairbrush, her toothbrush and some face cleanser. An ache of wanting pierced her heart. She closed her eyes and saw nothing but Tyler. The ache uncurled through her chest, prompting a mix of love and reverence toward the image now held in her heart of a man who was a devoted, tender Christian full of a giving spirit. She kept her eyes closed, going still as his handsome features swirled into even richer clarity, drawing her further into a world she hadn't dared to hope for, or dream of, until now.

She could almost taste him—feel him—in the escalating wind that moved through the room. Rolls of thunder rumbled, echoing upward through the valley in a somber vibration that literally moved against the house. Amy sat on the bed and promptly sank against its plush surface, stretching out while she continued to do battle against old demons while trying so hard to embrace new angels.

The bedroom door banged open, and Pyper entered the room at a run, charging toward the bed with happy gusto.

"Mama, I heard thunder! We're gonna have a storm! And I get to not be scared 'cause you'll be with me!"

Was it just Amy's imagination, or was Pyper picking up a southern twang after less than a week? The thought left her to grin while she grabbed for her daughter. "You bet I will. Come here, snug-a-bug."

Amy pulled her squirmy, giggling daughter onto the down comforter of the bed. They laid side by side, cushioned by feathery softness, both of them happy, for the time being, to simply look into one another's eyes and rest in contentment. Amy's mind slowly eased as rain came down in a soft downpour that played like a lullaby to her soul.

Yes, this whole contentment thing was contagious. It was addictive. Beautiful and beneficial. For the first time in ages, Pyper looked and acted as innocent and carefree as any five-year-old should. That fact applied a necessary balm to the long-standing scar across Amy's spirit.

All of a sudden, Pyper smiled big, and cupped her hand against Amy's cheek in a way that she always did when she simply wanted to connect and touch her mother, heart to heart. Her other hand was presently tucked beneath her chin.

"You like Tyler, huh, Mommy?"

"Yes. Yes I do."

The smile grew even bigger. "A really lot?" Pyper's eyes twinkled, alive with playful mischief—and the first signs of a little girl beginning to recognize matters of the heart. No sense hiding from the most important person in her life. That was another life-lesson Amy had learned the hard way.

"Yeah, Pyper. A really lot."

Pyper blinked a few times, her long, inky lashes fluttering a bit tiredly over eyes of palest, most luminous blue. "Me, too, Mommy." Pyper yawned, her eyes closing as she moved in close. Amy wrapped her arms tight around her daughter who drifted promptly to sleep.

Conversely, Amy came to life. Despite every doubt and fear, her heart began to race, beating in time to an influx of battered but stalwart hope.

❧❧

Pyper was down for the count, oblivious to the continuous strobes of lightning and the aftershocks of crackling energy that rippled through the air. Rain intensified; the rooftop drumbeat a strong and steady pound. Amy glanced at the bedside clock and groaned softly when she registered the time. At just after midnight, she was nowhere near the realm of sleep. The hissing voices of doubt kept crowding in.

Old demons, or new angels—what's it going to be, Maxwell?

Tyler deserves better than the damaged spirit you present, doesn't he? And what about Pyper? Amy, you can't possibly consider *pulling her into yet another new version of life, in a place that will remove her from everything, and everyone, that's familiar. Get a grip on this situation before it runs you over!*

Then, a new thought crept in, pushing more disruptive ripples against her psyche: she hadn't heard from Mark in ages—not since the divorce—but perhaps all it would take to make a desperate man reemerge is finding out his ex-wife and daughter were now an important part of Tyler Brock's life. A media push of interest and excitement, especially if they emerged as a couple, would put her past under intense scrutiny. Not only would her battles with abuse and an alcoholic husband come to the fore, they would be broadcast everywhere. How would that affect Pyper? What if Mark picked up on the idea of trying to stake an exploitive claim on their daughter?

That's why we pray.

The simple phrase she had exchanged with Tyler rolled through her troubled mind. Amy tried hard to find the words; all that came was a sense of devastation. A reconciliation of her life with Tyler's refused to materialize, no matter how hard she petitioned God.

There was just no way to remain in this idyllic world and relationship. No way at all.

Giving up on sleep that refused to come, Amy slipped out of bed as carefully as possible. She padded across the floor and looked outside for a moment, wondering what she could do to doze off and leave all that negativity behind.

She had never tried the warm-milk antidote, but decided to give it a go. She moved with light steps down the darkened stairwell, tip-toeing her way to the kitchen. By now, she was familiar enough with the layout to pull open a lower cabinet door and fish out a small saucepan. Next, she lifted a jug of milk from the refrigerator and poured.

Amy lit the burner beneath the pan.

"Storm keeping ya up?"

She gasped and nearly upended the saucepan. She turned fast, instantly nervous, and took a hard swallow at the vision before her. Sleep-tousled hair, a rumpled, plain white t-shirt and black sweats were an absurdly adorable combination on Tyler. He yawned, walking into the kitchen nonplussed...and barefoot.

Amy's muscles went tight; need slid into place with unraveling speed and efficiency. She fumbled with the cap of the milk jug and cleared her throat when she brushed slowly past Tyler to return it to the fridge. But then, his arrival, and what might be behind it, prompted her to put her sensual cravings into simmer mode rather than boil. "Are you having trouble sleeping, too? Would you like me to make you some?"

Tyler gave a small shake of his head. "Nah. Thanks, though. You OK?"

"Yeah. Just a little restless I guess. Couldn't quite settle for some reason."

"My fault, maybe? I didn't mean to rip open your heart tonight. You comfortable enough?"

His earnestness touched her heart, and made her smile when she looked into his eyes. They struck her as being a touch sleep dusted. And he was so cute…

The simmering ratcheted upward again. "I'm fine, don't worry. Sorry if I woke you."

"No problem. I've been sleeping light the last few days." He moved to the spot next to her and peeked into the pot where bubbles began to lift upward and pop.

"Thinking about Kellen's representation offer? Your work?"

He shrugged. "Partly. Mostly it's just…" He shrugged again and the t-shirt bunched and flexed around his shoulders, which were broad and perfectly toned. Amy drifted into that image as he paused. How easily she could imagine the feel of his warm skin, the texture of downy hair and sinew. "Mostly it's you and Pyper. Having the two of you here."

Amy centered back on the conversation in a hurry. "Oh?"

"It's a good thing—a very good thing—but it's–it's complicated."

"How so?" His comments took her aback. Now she wanted answers.

He moved in close enough to rest a hand against her arm and give it a squeeze. "It's important to me. It's like a picture of everything I've wanted for so long.

But it's going to be over within a few days. I don't want it to be. Please — tell me it won't be."

Amy took a breath, lost in his eyes as a breaking point came and went, dealt with by nothing more than the power of her heart.

She found enough courage to remain close to him. "I don't want it to be, either," she whispered. "You didn't want our first kiss to be a kiss goodbye." *It's not goodbye. Not yet.* Amy trembled. "Kiss me, Tyler."

She saw his surprise. Wishing on a hundred dreams, she looked at him with wide, but steady eyes. Waiting.

"This isn't casual for me, Amy. Never has been. Never could be. You understand that, right?"

His warning didn't trouble her at all. Slowly she nodded. Her world blurred at the edges with a delicious warmth and dizziness, with feathers going wild against her senses. "That's why I want it so much. If you do, too, that is…"

Tyler breathed out. He lowered his head until his forehead rested against hers. "Only since I was seventeen years old."

He slid his hand against her neck; not once did his eyes leave hers. Amy took strength from that. He cupped her face so gently, with such soft, reverent care that her eyes fluttered closed, and she sighed. Tyler's lips skimmed softly against her neck, her cheeks, her chin, in a smooth, tantalizing glide. His caress tickled her skin. He continued to nuzzle and seek, and Amy gave a pleasured, almost desperate sound. She could think only of his kiss — *their* kiss.

"Remember," he murmured against her now trembling, waiting mouth, "you asked."

He claimed her lips fully, exploring her in touch

and taste as his fingers slid down her arm. The modest covering of her long sleeved pajama top didn't diminish the warmth, or the tingling. Tyler pulled her snug against him as the kiss continued, blooming amidst a love that had been denied for far too long.

Amy sank against him and gave over to the moment. His lips were supple, sweetly flavored. Desire sang through her bloodstream, but she trusted him implicitly. The truth that she rested within the circle of his arms, her entire universe reduced to Tyler and the dimly illuminated kitchen—their two hearts beating an erratic tattoo—left Amy to soar.

Out of necessity, the moment ended way too quickly. Incrementally Tyler tempered the kiss, reducing the long and lush exploration to soft, sweet repeats of a connection that stirred heat and longing into a heady flow.

Finally, he leaned back, casting her a long look. "That…was *well* worth the wait."

She blushed furiously and looked down, toeing at a seam in the ceramic floor. But suddenly, up rose the Amy of old. She looked into Tyler's eyes head on. "We came close. Once."

Tyler grinned, but the gesture was touched by sadness, and a haunting sense of loss. "Most terrifying sixty-or-so seconds of my life."

She didn't buy into the humor. Instead, she used a soft touch to stroke his chin, then his jaw. "I'm so sorry."

He shook his head, combing his fingers very gently, very slowly through the loose strands of her hair. "For what?"

"For making you doubt that your love, your show of affection, wouldn't be accepted. I wanted you to kiss me that day. Did you know that? Did you sense how much I needed everything you offered? Mostly I'm sorry for all the time I wasted. For how stupid I was in not seeing the truth—that the best thing in the world was right in front of me."

"Honey, do *not* go back down that road, OK?" He leaned a hip against the counter and slid his hand against her arm lightly, automatically. He closed the distance between them once more to nuzzle her cheek for a moment and give her a kiss with a sigh before backing up, and looking her straight in the eyes. "There's one thing I know to be true in my heart: God's timing is perfect. If we'd tried this all those years ago, it may have ended differently. It might not have worked. We weren't the same people back then."

But he was. He truly was the same caring, wide-open person she had always known. Amy glided her fingers through the fall of his hair. "Not much change took place in your case," she murmured. "You were good to the core then, and you've stayed that way."

In the instant that followed, Tyler's eyes clouded, darkening with his own inner turmoil. Amy turned off the heat on the burner and poured milk into a mug to take with her to bed. She knew the pattern of his thoughts without benefit of words. He was in his own quandary—this one of a professional nature, and it required resolution before too long. Tyler Brock, one of the straightest, most forthcoming people she knew, faced heavy temptation—a pathway to mega-success, mega-exposure and perhaps a mega-loss of his soul.

Or not…depending…

After caressing his cheek, Amy lifted up on tiptoe and kissed him once more, taking her time with the gesture. The ready way he answered the summons and held her caused a pulse rush.

"G'night, Tyler," she finally whispered. Regret layered her tone. An intense need had built ever since he entered the kitchen, a need that would only know surcease when she belonged to him in fullness and a mutual, life-giving commitment. Tears stung her eyes.

As if such a thing could ever even happen.

15

The next morning, Tyler rose from bed following a long, invigorating stretch. Outside the bedroom window, a view of the distant mountains greeted him. He looked out, over the curving bowl of a verdant green valley presently blanketed by a thick layer of ghostly white fog. The view never failed to take his breath away. Air-cooled vapors blanketed the base of the mountains, swirling upward and dissipating beneath the rays of a golden sun just rising above the peaks.

After a quick shower, he changed into shorts and a polo shirt. He jogged down the stairs, drawn by an unexpected smell: cooking meat. It seemed RuthAnne was already active in the kitchen. God love her and bless her, he thought with a sincere sense of devotion.

Upon entering the kitchen, however, he came upon a surprise. Dressed in shorts and a t-shirt that were covered by an apron, Amy stood at the stove, fussing over a couple of pots. His heart pumped; a thick, heady thrill worked through him at the natural way she moved through his home, and his life.

She greeted him with a distracted, adorably frazzled glance. Tyler moved in on her from behind and lifted the lid of the largest pot. Steam curled upward, as did the tantalizing aroma of simmering chicken and seasoned sauce. He breathed in appreciatively. "RuthAnne's been busy this morning."

"No. I have." Amy took advantage of his lid retrieval to dump in an array of fresh vegetables— carrots, celery, green pepper, onion, corn, and cubed potatoes.

"Really? This is her classic. How'd you get her to give you the recipe?"

Amy spooned broth over the meat and veggies. She stirred slowly. "I love RuthAnne. She's great, and very generous."

Tyler replaced the lid and Amy set the now-empty strainer in the sink. "I wanted to do something special for you. To say thank you for everything you've done for us. When I explained, she surrendered the recipe."

Her subdued mood troubled him. Amy toweled off her hands and untied the apron she wore so she could pull it over her head and hang it on a nearby wall peg. He thought about her comments from last night and adrenaline spiked through his system, performing a dance that prickled against his arms and rang in his ears. He walked over to the counter and slid a knife from the wooden holder. Armed, he diced up a few more vegetables, preparing cauliflower and broccoli by separating the heads and rinsing them in the strainer.

"Pyper and I have been having a great time with you, Tyler," Amy continued. "To be honest, I don't remember ever feeling as happy and just…good…as I have during the times I've spent with you lately." She lifted the lid again and resumed stirring, occupying herself with unnecessary business. Tyler carried his prepped vegetables to the pot and slid them in while trying not to let his imagination get the best of him. But then, Amy gave a sad sigh. "I don't want to lose this."

"Then we won't." His answer contained a calculated force of conviction and finality. After last night, he didn't want her thinking about goodbye. Not yet. There was still time enough left on the clock to convince her that a conclusion to this week together would—and should—be nothing but temporary. So, he moved ahead with his own thoughts and ideas. "Did you happen to bring anything kinda dressy?" he asked in an offhand manner.

Amy went to the sink and began cleaning dishes. "I brought a dress and a pair of heels. Why?"

"That'll be fine."

She tilted her head, and gave him an expectant look. "Fine for what?"

"Well, see, my record label is throwing a promotional party tomorrow night." Tyler let pleasure run free through his system. He couldn't resist the idea of attending a glitzy function with Amy at his side. He crossed behind her and whisked a baby carrot from the extras that were stacked on a nearby cutting board. "Want to come? It's going to be at the Grand Ballroom of the Hermitage Hotel."

Amy's most immediate response was wide eyes.

"I'd love for you to be there with me. You'll get to see some of my band mates again, and you'll also meet Kellen Rossiter."

"Really?" That piqued her interested, but he detected her disquiet as well. Unless Tyler misread the slight furrow to her brow, and the hesitance in her eyes, Amy seemed a touch intimidated by the idea.

"Kellen will be recruiting. I'm sure I can line up RuthAnne to take care of Pyper for us so we can indulge in a five-star meal beforehand, then some necessary schmoozing and networking. And on

Saturday—"

Amy laughed. "I see there's no rest for the wicked in your world. Is that the point you're trying to make?"

Tyler sighed dramatically. "On Saturday," he tried again, "you and Pyper can spend some time at the recording studio with me. After the way she enjoyed playing on the piano, I think Pyper will go nuts for it, actually."

"No question about that. Sounds like fun."

"I'm putting together a couple of new songs I wrote that I think will be part of the next release. I want to get some preliminary recordings down. The studios are in downtown Nashville, so after we record, we can play tourist."

Amy shook her head, obviously still overwhelmed, but less taut in the shoulders; her answering smile appeared genuine. "OK, I'm officially impressed."

"No need to be. It's just a job."

"Yeah. OK." She spared him a wry look on her way to recheck the bubbling pot.

Tyler grabbed an extra celery stick this time and crunched away. He arched a brow. "So are you in?"

Amy lifted her hands in mock surrender. "Ah…sure. Why not?"

She stepped close. Tyler reached out easily and drew her into the circle of his arms, which tucked neatly around her waist. He rested his cheek against her hair and gave an inner sigh of delight. "Thanks. I'm actually looking forward to it now."

❧

The sounds of a creaking floorboard and carpet-cushioned footsteps at the top of the stairs drew Tyler's attention. Paused in the landing, he stood before a picture mirror where he adjusted the knot and fall of a silk tie. He looked up, and could do nothing but stare.

Amy gave him a fast, hesitant look, and then walked slowly down the staircase. She was a vision in delicate, pale blue lace. Lined beneath by fluid, darker satin, the v-necked, knee-length dress moved like it was a part of her. The color drew his focus to her fair, creamy skin, her large blue eyes.

The overall impact left his throat dry and knocked him straight back to those enchanted moments in high school when he had imagined sharing just such a moment with her. Now, like then, his knees went weak.

"I, umm, I hired a driver for tonight. A limo. It's out front. It'll be easier that way." He was babbling. He nearly burst out laughing at the crazy thought that crossed his mind: he somehow felt like he should have gotten her a corsage.

He saw her intimidation return when she tilted her head, and looked up at him almost plaintively. Tyler thought, once more, about the badlands she had traveled in their years apart and the changes life's imprint had left on her formerly free, confident spirit.

"A limo? That's deluxe."

Tyler took her hands in his and gave her arms a gentle shake. "Nah, it's not deluxe, just easier to navigate. There's going to be a lot of traffic out front of The Hermitage." He looked deliberately into her eyes, and did his best to telegraph assurance through a smile. "You OK?"

She nodded, but the gesture was too fast, and she looked away.

"Do me a favor—relax. Relax and enjoy being treated well. Sometimes it's OK to be the belle of the ball, and to me, that's what you'll always be. I want you to have fun tonight."

He touched her cheek to punctuate that statement. Amy had pinned up her hair; a number of tiny, sparkling clips held it in place. Blonde curls swirled and danced around her neck, making him want to reach up—just for a second or two—and twist a satiny strand around his fingertip to enjoy the texture.

Amy smoothed her fingers beneath the lapel of his suit coat. "You look great, by the way."

"Yeah? Thanks, because you wrote the book. I'm just tryin' to keep pace."

Pink color bloomed through her cheeks. Amy glanced into the great room just beyond. There, Pyper was on her stomach, scissor-kicking her legs and watching television. RuthAnne sat in a rocking chair and worked on her cross-stitch pattern that was gradually taking the form of a flower-filled meadow. Once Tyler realized Amy was comfortable and satisfied by the homey scene they would leave behind, he offered his arm. "Are you ready?"

Amy nodded, taking hold and letting him lead the way.

❧⊰❦

Exclamation Point Records had pulled out all the stops for tonight's networking event. Tyler kept a guiding hand on Amy's waist as they joined the crowd that milled through the wide-open space of the Grand Ballroom. During the span of his five years in Nashville, Tyler had never visited the Hermitage

Hotel. The Nashville landmark was impeccable—the definition of elegance and old-world influence. Not a bad underscore to the idea of promoting a Christian music label to the agents, producers, and performers who would help the company grow.

Directing their progress toward the spot where Dave and Rebecca stood, Tyler left Amy in their care while he went to the bar to pick up a pair of soft drinks. He entered the line. While he waited, he nodded at a few people he knew; he smiled into the lenses of a few cameras that flashed and popped. The ballroom was lush and extravagant, featuring ornate ceilings with deep, textured coves punctuated by dark, walnut paneling. Elaborately framed paintings accented the walls.

The line moved forward, and he centered on the people around him once more. That's when he realized Kellen Rossiter stood just ahead, at the head of the queue.

The bartender greeted Kellen with a courteous smile. "What can I get for you, sir?"

"Two tonics with lime, please."

Tumblers were filled promptly. Tyler waited just behind him, but moved close enough to enter Kellen's field of vision and give him a questioning look. "Not a drinker?"

Kellen shrugged. "If I drank at even half the events I'm forced to attend, I'd be out of control, so, I don't drink at all. I like to keep a clear head."

Tyler couldn't help but smile. "Impressive."

"No. Necessary."

"Mm-hmm" Tyler ordered two colas—one for him, one for Amy—but he longed for the snappy spice of his favorite—ginger ale.

Kellen took a generous sip of his beverage, eyeing the crowd. "Nicely done, by the way. Your girlfriend? She's stunning."

"Nothing gets past you, Rossiter," he jabbed lightly, giving his would-be agent a territorial grin. "And keep your distance."

"No problem. I'd never interfere in your potential happiness as a well-grounded Christian recording artist. Given the chance, I could sell the idea of a solidly committed and caring singer by the mile. It's an appealing image. Besides, my wife wouldn't approve."

Tyler was about to take a sip of his drink, but stopped midway. Kellen. Married. The fact added a new dimension to the man. When Kellen lifted his glass again and drank, Tyler considered the second tumbler and took note of the wide, gold wedding band, noticing the ring for the first time. "Is she here?"

"In the same circle as your girlfriend, as a matter of fact. Right over there." Kellen gestured and Tyler took note of a beautiful, petite-framed woman dressed in jewel green. She had softly waved, auburn hair, gentle curves, and the face of an angel.

"Nicely done yourself, Rossiter."

"I'm keenly aware of the fact. Come on over and meet her. Juliet's heard a lot about you. Besides, I'd like to meet this famous photographer and blast from the past of yours."

Tyler gaped. "Honestly. How do you *know* all this stuff?"

Kellen's smile was hard to refuse. "I'm good at my job. I connect dots, do some research, and *voila*...a picture comes to life."

Tyler chuckled. This guy was unique to his experience. *Very* unique. "You never give up, do you?"

"Nope."

They joined their group just in time to hear Dave filling Amy in on the history of the hotel. "…yeah — even presidents come here. Kennedy, Roosevelt, Wilson and Nixon — they've all slept at The Hermitage. Plus, from Al Jolson to Al Capone, all kinds of celebs have stayed here, too."

Tyler stepped into the circle of his friends. "Jolson and Capone. That kinda covers the spectrum of human endeavor, now doesn't it?"

"For better, and for worse." Dave greeted the newcomer to their group with a quirked grin and an arched brow. "Kellen. It's good to see you. I've already decided your wife here doesn't deserve you. You lucked out in the marriage department."

Juliet Rossiter swatted at Dave's arm, but wore a large smile. "Stop it!"

"Tell me something I don't know. It's good to see you, too, Dave. Juliet, here you go, love." He handed his wife her drink, which she accepted with a smile that moved straight from her eyes and into Kellen's. Something in the natural, easy intimacy of their interaction left Tyler compelled, and intrigued.

"Dave's not just a world-class tour manager. He's a history geek, too," Tyler spoke, recapturing the conversation at hand.

"Which is why I love Nashville so much, hot-shot."

Tyler handed Amy her drink. "Amy, meet Kellen Rossiter. Kellen, this is Amy Maxwell."

"Great to meet you, Amy."

"And Amy, Kellen is truly my better half," Juliet interjected, her green eyes sparkling when she looked up at her husband. "I was telling Amy how much I wish I had an eye for imagery and photography like she does. What a wonderful gift."

Amy received Kellen's handshake. "And obviously I'm enjoying getting to know your wife. I understand she's a native to Nashville, like Dave."

Kellen tucked into Juliet's side in an automatic way, wrapping an arm around her waist. "Meanwhile, I followed my heart to the south from California. I'm a Los Angeles transplant."

Paul Jacobs, president of Exclamation Point Records took his position behind a podium on a dais at the front of the room. Conversations came to a standstill. Opening remarks prompted people to move to their seats, each of which were identified by name cards crafted in calligraphy. Gift bags prompted Tyler to lean close to Amy's ear. "Enjoy the swag. I remember at last year's event there was a pretty nice selection of treats."

Kellen and Juliet settled in across from them. Dave and Rebecca arrived as well and sat down. Expansive and oval-shaped, the table they shared featured rose-hued linens, simple bone china, crystal goblets and silver flatware. Tyler took in the details and atmosphere but sat back to listen as formal proceedings began. His attention alternated between Amy, who watched with an expression of subdued awe, and Kellen, who kept his eyes trained on the dais and his arm draped loosely along the back of Juliet's chair.

The agent managed to make his interest known, while at the same time maintaining a comfortable distance.

Media members swarmed at the beginning of the program, snapping pictures at a fast clip. Tyler noticed that Amy tracked the progress of the reporters. She looked bewildered by the degree of attention. As people moved through the room, a number of producers, back-up singers, technicians, and label execs from Exclamation Point stopped by to pay Tyler a quick, though discreet greeting.

Amy leaned close. "I feel like Alice falling down the rabbit hole."

Tyler regarded her intently. The comment didn't resonate with humor. He could tell by her reserved, closed-off posture that she honestly felt like she had entered an alternate universe.

Disquiet over Amy and confusion over Kellen, built as the evening progressed.

∂∽∾∾

A couple hours later, his thoughts tumbling, Tyler left the fading party behind. He walked into the lobby, waiting for Amy to return from a visit to the restroom. Kellen had made only one overture about representation all night—that joke at the bar about selling Tyler via commitment to a happy relationship. Kellen didn't push; he hadn't hovered. Tyler appreciated those facts, but at the same time, came away perplexed, wondering about the agent's lack of pressure.

Then there was Amy's reaction to the evening. The mood he sensed from her wasn't at all reassuring. She had been warm; she engaged easily when spoken to, but beyond that, she kept to herself, cataloguing the events of the evening in a manner Tyler could only describe as shuttered. He intended to ask her about that.

Beyond the glass doors of the hotel entrance, he

spied a lineup of limousines. A few stray photographers milled about. The glamour of the hotel lobby drew his focus. Italian marble floors, a vaulted ceiling created of stained glass and overstuffed, luxurious furniture all vied for his attention, drawing him into a world he could most definitely admire, but never dive in to with complete abandon. The whole evening had affected him that way. A night of glitz and glamour was one thing; living in the constant glare of a spotlight was quite another, which was a new point to ponder.

As the thought evolved, a conversation nearby earned his interest; one of the voices he heard belonged to Kellen Rossiter.

"Rossie. You're headed out, too?"

Kellen's laugh reached Tyler. Only, the laugh didn't seem warm, or overly humorous. "I hate being called Rossie, which you know full well, Clay."

"Why else do you think I'd use it? You know how it goes—agent to agent nothing delights me like needling the competition."

Tyler stayed out of range for the time being and watched the proceedings. Kellen stood near the entrance of the lobby, chatting with a short, pudgy man who presently chewed on an unlit cigar. In vague terms, Tyler remembered him from the party. Kellen kept an eye on both the ladies' room and the line of cars outside. Waiting for his wife, Tyler assumed. If he recalled correctly, as the party disbursed, Juliet had headed out with Amy.

"Juliet's getting tired and there's no need to overstay my welcome."

"Suppose not, especially since you seem to have achieved your agenda for the night: charming Tyler

Brock. Everybody knows you're after him in a big way. Seems you've made inroads. Have you clinched the deal yet?"

"What *deal*?" Though smooth in tone, Kellen's voice carried with it a slice of tension that spelled danger to Tyler's ears.

"The deal to add Tyler to your client list." Clay's reply was unapologetic and blunt.

"I'd love to represent him, but he's not an agenda item. I came here to check up on Exclamation Point's progress. The label is up and coming. Great portfolio of talent."

Tyler still kept to the side, and away from their immediate notice; his brows pulled together. Kellen's discretion and tact won Tyler's appreciation— especially when Clay continued to push.

"A great portfolio of talent that includes Tyler Brock, right?"

"Yeah. So?"

The simple two-word response resounded with a steely warning. Tyler waited, expectant and on edge.

"Well, I guess I'm just a little curious is all. I mean, why are you hinging yourself on Bible-belt performers, Rossiter?"

"Because the music is good, and the message is even better. Since that equals a win/win situation, sure I'm exploring the genre. What about that equation doesn't make sense to you?"

Kellen's tone was casual, but once again Tyler sensed something just beneath. Something battle-ready and challenging that he could appreciate, and completely relate to.

"Hey, easy on there. Don't be so defensive, I—"

"I'm not being defensive. You're the one who

asked. I'm just straightening out a misguided perception."

Kellen's companion shrugged in a show of magnanimous tolerance. "Whatever, whatever. It's not a bad idea, really, to practice inclusiveness, especially when it comes to the Christian sect."

Tyler bristled at the demeaning comment. He made ready to step forward, and make his presence known.

"What I'm doing isn't about a *sect.*" Kellen answered sharply. "I believe in the music, and the artists I'm coming to know."

The words stopped Tyler from interrupting. His footsteps stuttered to a stall.

Again came a shrug from the other guy, this one dismissive. "Gotta give you credit. You've always been ahead of the curve when it comes to pushing trends and pulling in the talent to do it. You've always known what buttons to push, but I have the feeling this will be your first stumble. After all, squeaky clean and righteous? Not sure how great that'll sell these days. Too bland. Not enough intensity and drive to draw in that young, sexy demographic we're all fighting to win."

Kellen's rumbling chuckle drifted through the lobby. "Well, to me, the idea of eternity is pretty intense, and can offer that *demographic* plenty of drive when given the right platform. I'm ready to give Christian music, and its more promising artists, the push they deserve."

Absorbed by the scene, Tyler shook his head and gave a soft snort when he watched Clay sneer in a placating, completely insincere manner. "Good luck with that. Well, there's my car. See you later."

Kellen didn't reply, continuing to wait for Juliet. That's when Tyler finally re-found his footing. He crossed the lobby in a few short strides. "Kellen."

If perturbed by the previous exchange, Kellen didn't show it. He offered a warm smile and a nod. "Hey, Tyler."

Kellen, he now noticed, carried two gift bags, his and Juliet's. Since Tyler did the same for himself and Amy, they shared a grin and looked in the direction of the restrooms.

"Amy and Juliet really hit it off," Tyler said.

"They did. It was a fun night. I'll make sure I say as much to Paul."

"Nice name drop," Tyler teased.

Kellen, still being Kellen, was on the job. Paul was the president of Exclamation Point Records.

Kellen's features went stormy. "You know? Sometimes it's a battle to even try to do what I dream of. I wonder if you understand that. I'm not *after* anything. It's just that I see tremendous potential in you and the other artists here at Exclamation Point. I see potential in the music you create. A potential I'd like to encourage. Paul's a friend, that's all, so I intend to thank him for a nice evening."

Though taken aback by Kellen's strident response, Tyler understood the undercurrent. Kellen's mood obviously stemmed from residual steam that had built up following the previous exchange. "You know what, Kellen? I get that now. I really do." Tyler took note of the skeptical expression Kellen wore, and went serious in a hurry. "That's why I'd like to invite you to a recording session Saturday morning. After that, let's plan to talk for a bit."

Kellen went still, then he nodded, studying Tyler

with knitted brows and narrowed eyes. "I'll be there, but why the generosity?"

"Because you recognize a genre, not a *sect*. Because you recognize the message in the music. I appreciate that." Tyler waited a beat, watching realization dawn in Kellen's eyes. He gave Kellen a knowing grin.

The women joined them, and Tyler tucked his hand into Amy's as she bid the Rossiters goodnight. "Juliet, it was a pleasure to meet you. Kellen, the session is set up for Saturday morning at eleven o'clock. Studio B."

"I'll see you then."

16

Surprisingly enough, it was the swag bag that re-released a floodgate of doubts for Amy. Especially the 14 Karat gold bracelet she had discovered inside, tucked into a black velvet jeweler's box placed artfully amidst sparkling tissue paper. Also included were a myriad of high-end goodies like designer label cosmetics and generous gift cards to apparel stores she normally wouldn't tempt herself by going near, let alone actually patronize. The bracelet now decorated her wrist. Amy touched the simple, shimmering cross that dangled from the chain; it captured the morning sunlight that poured in through a nearby window. She slouched at the small dining table in Tyler's kitchen, lost in thought.

Where is this really headed? Is this nothing more than a week-long voyage down a primrose path leading to a mirage?

Amy's entire being repelled the idea, even as practical logic snaked its way into existence all over again, pushing hard against each of her newfound joys and a tenuous hope for what the future could hold.

Following last night's "A-List" style celebration for Exclamation Point Records, the prospect of media speculation, and a spotlight being shined on the stains of her past, continued to gain traction. Tyler was making headway into both Christian and mainstream recording markets. That was tremendous. And much deserved. But, what would fans, and media members, think of him being involved with a divorcee who coped with life as a single working mom following the end of a marriage marred by both physical abuse and alcoholism? Worse than that, what would the glare of a spotlight mean for an unsuspecting innocent like Pyper?

Additionally, thoughts of Mark crept into the corners of her heart. Would he catch wind of her relationship? Would he reemerge and exert pressure on her, via Pyper, in order to manipulate or extort? Certainly in such a case Tyler would step in, ever a source of strength and support. But Amy didn't want him to have to contend with such an event. He didn't deserve additional pressure and concerns about his image, his work—and his heart.

Gossip-laden headlines—based upon fact or fiction—would not bode well for Tyler and his forward momentum. Plus, constant scrutiny, and the idea of tarnishing Tyler's life in any way, gave Amy a lot to consider.

She didn't doubt Tyler's depth of emotion. To do so was impossible. Nor did she question her own veracity of spirit. How could she? Guided by heartfelt sincerity and tenderness, Tyler drew them into the loving circle of his life with an expert's precision. But those facts didn't keep her from having to face a colder, harder truth: life with Tyler Brock would take her, and Pyper, far from the stability of the life they had worked so hard to build back in Michigan.

The Ruth and Boaz analogy Amy had embraced just one short week ago didn't seem to make nearly as much sense any longer. Why? Because the story of Ruth and Boaz didn't feature the life of a child—a child who desperately needed a solid and comfortable foundation.

Here, in Tennessee, they were happy, certainly, but upheaval was upheaval. Together, she and Pyper had struggled through so much life change that additional uprooting wasn't a viable option. Especially when coupled with the intrusive speculation of tabloids and the thousands of media outlets clambering for details on the lives of celebrities—the racier and more controversial, the better. Several aspects of her relationship with Tyler would feed that quest.

Amy groaned aloud and balled her breakfast napkin into a tight wad of paper. Would a relationship be in Tyler's best interests? He might think so. In return, she might long for just such a connection. In reality, however, "Tyler and Amy" would be a sticky, scrutinized model. Most likely, the situation would turn ugly for all three of them. That was a circumstance Amy couldn't accept, nor in any way reconcile.

Fantasies involving Tyler and a picture-perfect life now struck her as impossible.

So, with forty-eight hours left on the clock in Franklin, Amy arose from her seat in the kitchen to a tune of growing discord and sadness. She took her dishes to the sink and rinsed them, weakened at the shoulders by sullen thoughts and an ache of tiredness that filled her soul.

Falling asleep last night had been a solitary experience; before the record label event, Pyper had proudly announced she wanted to give *her* room a try. Amy recognized the decision had much to do with the plethora of goodies stored there, and the gauzy netting of the canopy bed, which simply begged for a little girl to curl up beneath its protection and dream of glorious fairytales. Solitude proved a double-edged sword for Amy—peaceful, certainly, but echoing with the thoughts and doubts that churned through her mind.

At breakfast this morning, RuthAnne had joined them, and the meal struck Amy like the precious pieces of a family unit. Determinedly she rebuked that thought as fast as it arose, although outwardly she remained as warm and upbeat as possible.

Now, with everyone disbursed into the call of the day ahead, she stewed while she stored dishes in the washer.

Presently, Tyler showered and dressed. Amy, Tyler, and Pyper had decided to spend today at a slow pace and keep close to home so Pyper could play, and the adults could simply relax. The interlude was soothing, but Amy remained unsettled. Her emptiness correlated directly to a lack of confidence she couldn't quell, or ignore. Not when all of the arrows in her life pointed away from the truest call of her heart.

For dinner, they went to Puckett's, a Tennessee institution with standard American fare, live music, and a country-style atmosphere that roused the embers of her doused mood. After praying over their meal, Tyler dug in. "Tomorrow's recording session will probably take a couple of hours." Tyler helped himself to a stash of fries then bit into his hamburger. "Are you sure you don't mind coming along? I really want you with me, so you can see how everything comes together, but it might be a little boring."

The question cut into her thoughts, which had strayed once again. Amy gave herself an internal shake, drawn back to the appealing hubbub of dining out at a restaurant full of happy energy. Conversations swirled, glassware and dinner utensils chinked and clanged, footsteps creaked against worn wooden floor planks. Pyper swung her legs, errantly connecting with Amy's calf from time to time. Pyper was lost to the atmosphere of Puckett's, happily absorbing the crowd and some well-played banjo music.

"I can't wait to hear what you're working on. It'll be anything but boring." Amy smiled at him and forced herself into a more proper, upbeat demeanor. She propped her elbows on the tall, window-side table where they sat. Bathed by the golden light of late afternoon sunset, people milled through the streets, enjoying a gorgeous summer evening. She let the beauty of the scene seep into her soul.

Pyper chewed on her grilled cheese sandwich and looked up at Tyler with wide, pleading eyes. "Me, too? Can we sing together too, Tyler? Please?"

Amy cringed, preparing to interject at once, but before she could speak, Tyler rested his hand on top of hers and gave a warning squeeze that kept Amy silent for the time being.

"I need to record a couple songs with my group, but I'll see what we can arrange. Maybe we can lay down a track of you and me playin' Chopsticks."

Pyper gasped. "And singing our ABC's, too? We're really good at that."

He laughed and tweaked her nose. "We sure are, sugar beet. I think that's doable."

She nodded hard. "And know what else? I decided something. Something important."

Amy braced herself for just about anything. "What's that?"

"I'm gonna be a singer when I grow up. Just like Tyler."

The statement worked right past every defense Amy possessed. And stirred up a world full of emotions: good and bad.

∂∾⫯

On their way out of the restaurant, Pyper weaved through a cluster of customers who had just arrived at Puckett's. Amy watched after her daughter while Pyper charged toward the window display of a toy store they had passed on their way into downtown Franklin. Pyper leaned against the cement sill of the shop, looking inside with dreamy eyes.

"Pyper has certainly taken a major-league turn when it comes to you, Tyler. I'm glad for that." The automatic way he reached for her hand warmed Amy's heart despite the cold of her misgivings.

"I am, too. She's happy, don't you think? Confident."

"Yes. Definitely."

They meandered toward Pyper, down the length of a wide sidewalk dotted by ornate wrought iron street lamps, but then, Tyler's subtle tug on her hand brought Amy to a stop. "You know? The same can be said for her mom." His firm tone, the openness of his clear, hazel eyes, jammed any form of reply deep in her throat, right behind a thick swell of emotion.

She took a deep breath and swallowed. Removing her hand from his, she moved a few steps ahead. "I suppose so."

Pointedly Tyler stayed in place. When Amy attempted to venture forward once more, he held his ground. "Really? Is that all you're going to say?"

"What more do you want?" She wondered if the

words even registered over traffic noise and the chatter of passers by. She kept her lips from trembling by pressing them together.

"I want everything, Amy."

His intensity left her wanting distraction, so she looked toward her daughter. Pyper chatted with a little girl who joined her in admiring the toys that were framed in by a glass window. Happily occupied, they watched a twirling ballerina, admired a fully trimmed dollhouse and a chugging train. Amy resumed their stroll.

"What are you saying, Tyler? Seriously? That you want to marry me?"

"It's not an official proposal, no. Not yet. That moment will be much more precious, I promise you that. But ultimately, marriage is my intent, Amy. You wouldn't be here otherwise, and I think there's a big part of you that already knows that." He paused, letting her ingest that fact. "Why else would I bring you into my home, let you into the deepest parts of my life? I'm not casual when it comes to my heart, and I'm not cavalier about how I treat people. You know that better than anybody."

She shook her head slowly, meekly retreating from everything he offered. It was like a beautiful dream—therefore, it was also terrifying. "You can't possibly be serious." She swallowed, and her breathing went shallow. "Tyler, be rational. If you count Detroit, we've been together again for a week, and a handful of days."

"Is that all, Amy? Really?" His voice was deliberately soft. "You know? You might be the one who needs to be a little more rational right now."

"Don't you understand that I've just now begun to find myself again? After five long, horrible years? I'm starting to make my way back to a place where I can rebuild my life, but I don't know what can happen from here. Honestly. Look down the road and ask yourself if it'll work. Ask yourself if what you and I have is real, or if you're looking for nostalgia, and feelings, and a person you remember in far too idyllic a way, I'm not her anymore. And—"

He drew their steps to a close, capturing both her hands and holding her still. They stood in the middle of the Main Street sidewalk, in the rapidly darkening downtown. He cupped her face gently between his hands, brushing his thumbs against her cheeks. "Don't be afraid. Please. For *both* our sakes." His gaze traveled to Pyper, who bounded just ahead, this time captivated by another window display, this one full of sparkling crystal sculptures. "We're going to discuss this—at length—before you leave. For now, I make only one request. It's a plea from the depths of my heart."

Amy felt choked up, overly emotional. She gazed at him, vulnerable and helpless to everything she felt.

"For *all* our sakes, stop being afraid."

Let go. That was the underlying message, and she received it clearly, but not without a constricting dose of trepidation as well.

❧∾

When honesty is missing from your world, keep shining the truth.

When compassion is missing from your world, keep reaching out.

When love is missing from your world, keep showering love.

That's the only way to live true justice.

Because someone – somewhere – is:
Drowning in hate, drowning in fear, losing hope.

So never give up, and never give in –
Fight the fight you know you need to win.
Reflect what this world needs –
True justice.

Piano music flowed to a conclusion, fading into a silence that left the assemblage in the control booth awed. "Wow. Where did *that* come from?" Kellen Rossiter spoke for them all.

The ballad was a perfect blend of loving emotion laced by Christian value and dedication. Amy still tingled, awash in the moment. She wanted to answer the question by saying: *from the depths of an open, giving heart.* Kellen concluded the matter on his own. "The man has undeniable soul."

"Yeah, he does." Amy stood next to the powerhouse of an agent, who struck her as handsome, confident and smooth. "Know what I hope?"

Kellen waited on her.

"I hope and pray that nothing—and no one—ever tries to take it away from him."

Kellen's initial reaction was nothing more than a sidelong glance, accompanied by a quiet sigh. He absorbed her pointed look with grace, but not without a fight. A fire lit in his eyes. "Is it so hard to believe that I might have one, too?"

Amy shrugged, staring straight back. He didn't intimidate her. Not in the least. What did she have to lose? Not nearly as much as Tyler, and she wanted some form of assurance that he would be all right facing the glories—and tribulations—of widespread fame.

Once she was gone.

Kellen shook his head, looking back at Tyler who remained seated at the piano, studying music sheets with Rebecca. "In my own way, I'm trying to help evangelize, Amy. Whether you see that fact, and accept it, isn't up to me." His gaze returned to her, hardened by traces of hurt. "Tax collectors were the parasites of Jesus' day, so I can easily relate to Matthew's gospel. By living in a world of sin, he brought those who most needed Christ to the hem of His robe."

Startled, she folded her arms across her chest and watched the man. He looked back at Tyler, a smile just starting to reclaim his features. So, he was a Christian. Immersed in a world of glitz, materialism, fame, ambition and a never-ending quest for "more." Yet at the same time, he pushed for Christian artists. Pushed *hard*, in fact, if his courting of Tyler was any indication.

"Then don't hide a light as effective as yours under a bushel basket, Kellen. That's the other lesson Matthew learned. Be forthright about your faith, and you'll accomplish miracles. You'll help feed hungry souls out there."

He nodded toward Tyler, who stood from the piano and stretched, smiling and joking with his crew. Tyler seemed buoyed by the results of the session. "I like to think I already do." Kellen stepped out of the booth and slipped in to the recording area. "Hey, Tyler. Question for you."

"What's that?"

"The song you just sang, *True Justice*. Did it feel at all like a compromise?"

Tyler shrugged. Amy watched through the

glassed-in sound booth as he regarded Kellen in a puzzled way. "No."

Kellen extended his hand. "Then welcome to preaching in the mainstream. It's going to be a hit."

Tyler accepted the gesture then listened intently when Kellen continued. "Depending on what you come up with next, I easily see that as single number one. Single number two? Let's push a bit more into your Christian roots, something upbeat and unapologetic about bringing God—and God's grace—into the texture the song. I know you can do it, and do it without the feel of preaching—kinda like *Amazing Grace*. A song like that would make a great second release, and maintain the message you've always presented."

Slowly, *very* slowly, Tyler's expectant smile bloomed. "I can get behind that scenario."

Pyper sat next to the soundboard, twisting her chair back and forth. Holding her beloved fashion dolls on her lap, she bobbed her head and swayed the dolls in a dancing motion as she hummed the refrain of *True Justice*. Amy watched after her daughter who remained happily occupied. Pyper had been an angel during the session. As a treat, she had been given permission to record a CD of music with Tyler. A rousing rendition of Chopsticks and the ABC song were now preserved forever.

Amy's throat went full and tight. *Lord,* please *help me. How can I—how can we—leave this world behind tomorrow morning? I don't want to, but I don't see any other choice.*

Tears pricked and stung at the corners of her eyes. Telltale moisture built against her lashes, so she ducked her head to flick the droplets away with a fingertip.

"Mama, why are you crying?"

Amy sniffed quietly, grateful to be ignored by the others for the time being. "It's OK, Pyp. I'm just happy for Tyler is all. Very happy."

Appeased, Pyper straightened and gave a nod. "Me, too."

In a way, Amy wasn't fibbing to her daughter. Tyler was going to have an amazing, fulfilled life. Why did that realization leave her with such a sharp stab of pain?

The only answer she could come up with was love. And its impending loss.

17

Returning home from the studio, Tyler gave Amy some space. Now, however, it was time to confront the issues she had raised at dinner the other night about being uprooted, and finding a life in Tennessee. Without question, he needed to know where she stood before they parted in the morning.

After checking in with RuthAnne, Tyler walked into the kitchen while Pyper and Amy trotted upstairs. There, he assumed Amy would freshen up and Pyper would settle into her bedroom with its treasure trove of toys...and the freshly minted CD of her recording debut.

Tyler smiled at the memory of sitting next to Pyper on the piano bench in the studio and having more fun than he'd had in years doing what most people in his business might refer to as "goofing off." The joy in Pyper's eyes, the determination and enthusiasm she put into the music, told a completely different story than mere goofing off. This was life at its richest and most blessed.

Following a brief, closed-door meeting with Kellen Rossiter at the studio offices of Exclamation Point Records, Tyler let everything else drift away except Amy. They had spent the remainder of the day in Nashville, grabbing dinner at The Palm restaurant. Now, it was time to unearth the reasons for her recent preoccupation and establish a pathway for what would come next.

Lifting a glass pitcher from inside the refrigerator, Tyler poured two tall glasses of sweet tea. He walked out to the porch, already knowing Amy would gravitate there soon, to soak in the beauty of her final evening in Tennessee.

The unending cadence of cricket chirps and insect song placed him at rest. The air was stirred by soft, warm breezes; once again, the yard came alive with the sparkle of lightning bugs. He felt a wash of bittersweet pleasure when he considered the fact that, forevermore, lightning bugs would bring to mind the way Pyper had danced and twirled through his yard, and the way quiet southern nights had led to heart-to-heart conversations with the woman he loved—and always would.

He deposited Amy's glass on the table to the right of the porch swing, his on the table to the left. He sank onto the thick cushions, and waited for her. Only a few minutes passed before the screen door came open with a squeak. He turned in time to see Amy register the beverage offering and give him an appreciative smile.

"Thanks."

"Pleasure."

She joined him, and took a sip.

"Pyper settled in?"

"Yes. All she keeps talking about is being in the recording studio. You just might have created a protégée."

Tyler chuckled low in his throat. "Good. You see, it's all a part of my great, grand plan."

"Your great, grand plan?"

"Mm-hmm. My plan to keep you here."

Her expression went uncertain. Tense. Tyler leaned forward on his knees and looked directly into her eyes. Amy's lips quivered. She broke from their visual connection and leaned back. "I should have known…"

Tyler picked up on the subtle show of distance, and respected it, taking a drink of his tea. "Known what, honey?"

"I should have known how hard it would be to say goodbye." Her voice shook against those whispered words. "This is putting me through a wringer. What I feel for you? It's tearing me up inside. For my sake, and for Pyper's as well, I *really* should have seen that coming."

"Seems to me the answer is pretty simple." He reached out and brushed his thumb against the back of her hand where it rested on the cushion between them. Amy glanced away. "Don't leave. Not permanently, anyway." Tyler wanted to see her eyes, but when she had dipped her head, the fall of her hair hid her face. Undeterred, he slid a fingertip against her cheek, then slowly tucked her hair over her shoulder.

She finally lifted her gaze. Turbulence rolled off her in waves. She straightened and gave him a tight, brave smile. "I leave on Sunday morning, and by Monday morning you'll officially be represented by Kellen Rossiter. I still can't get over it. Obviously your meeting today went well, huh?"

So, he thought, *she wants to ignore a painful topic.* In compromise, Tyler decided to sidestep. For now, anyway. He leaned on his knees again, and stared knowingly into her eyes, silently agreeing to her conversation shift. "Yeah, it's official. His office is drafting an agreement. What do you think of him?"

Amy curled up her legs and turned toward him. "I think you'll end up being good for each other. He seems to have a lot of substance—once you work past the flash and polish."

The answer pleased him; it mirrored his own assumptions. Her answer validated the risk he knew he was taking. "Thanks."

She looked puzzled. "For what?"

"For being my sounding board. For being someone I can open up to and trust. You know me; you know what I'm all about. That's comforting in the face of uncertainty."

Amy gave his arm a squeeze, and she smiled. "I understand where you're coming from. Being at a crossroads is never easy."

"True enough. This episode has taught me to stop fighting and start reaching out instead. Are you finding that to be true as well?"

She went stiff. The smile all but faded. "My. What a pointed question."

In deliberate contradiction, Tyler leaned back and forced himself to relax. "Don't expect me to avoid what God's trying to show me. Especially when it comes to you."

"OK then, you want the truth?"

"Always."

Amy firmed her jaw. She pushed herself forward and looked at him intently. "Your pathway can't include me, or Pyper. How could it? How could we uproot ourselves and blend into something new, someplace different?"

Tyler didn't allow that verdict to fluster him. "Quite easily. In fact, we just discussed the recipe. Stop fighting and reach out. I'm not Mark, and I never will be."

His conviction was authentic. Absolute.

Amy's eyes flickered but her posture stayed tight. "I know that, Tyler, and that's not even my point." He opened his mouth to continue, but Amy sliced her hand through the air to stop him. "My point is this: Beyond the enormous life change that would happen logistically, there's an emotional aspect to it as well. I can see the tabloid headlines right now"—She snorted. Then, in dramatic fashion, Amy put up air quotes and assumed an announcer's voice—"'Christian rock phenom, Tyler Brock enters into a romantic relationship with a divorced single mother who's apparently on the mend and looking for love following the end of a marriage marred by alcohol abuse and domestic violence." She sank back against the side of the porch swing. "Do you really think your fans, and the media members who cover you and help shape your career are going to let that one slip by? I don't. How many of your fans are fundamentalist who frown on divorce? And what will happen when the find out my"—more air quotes—"'spiral into an abusive marriage' was caused by my philandering pre-marital sex?"

Tyler gasped. "Do you realize how badly that demeans what we feel for each other?"

"Tyler, it's not meant to demean. It's meant to be realistic! And then there's Mark! What if he reemerges, and tries to pressure you, or me, about Pyper? What if he exploits you, and me, for money, or some other form of support, in exchange for keeping away from me, and Pyper? These are legitimate concerns, Tyler. These are things we need to consider.

"My life is in Michigan. My *reality* is in Michigan.

It's what I know. It's what I've learned to handle, and it's what kept me, and Pyper, alive during the past year. Meanwhile, your life is here. Your career is here, and it's headed to wonderful places. Uprooting Pyper, uprooting myself, from everything that's familiar all over again and placing ourselves smack-dab in the middle of a harsh spotlight isn't a smart option right now—on a number of levels."

The peace of the evening evaporated like the day's humidity. Tyler stood abruptly from the swing. His steps turned into pacing. "Amy, do you think my life hasn't featured upheaval, and change, and challenge?"

"Of course it has, but—"

"No buts." His sharp interjection caused her to flinch, and Tyler winced. He hadn't meant to scare her, but he needed to get out how he felt. The clock was ticking away the last moments of their week together, and nothing was as important right now as giving voice to his heart. "I came to Tennessee with nothing but faith, and a dream. I gambled on Opry Bound with nothing but the sure knowledge that God would be in control of whatever happens. Now I'm facing an even more daunting circumstance—the danger that accompanies mass exposure and everything that goes along with it."

She blinked, folding her arms against her midsection. "Which is part of the point I'm trying to make. Don't you see? I won't be an asset to that part of your life. I'd do you more harm than good."

What?" Tyler spun on his heel and gaped at her. The exclamation hung in the air, tethered by strings of shock and disbelief. Across the space of the porch that now separated them a boiling edginess grew, but Tyler fought back anger as best he could. She didn't need anger. She needed clarity and understanding—and so did he. "Where is all this coming from, Amy? And is this why you were so remote last night?"

She nodded. "Yes, it is. I have to admit, the media gave me a lot to think about when it comes to privacy, and when it comes to what would be best for me and Pyper, and for you, and your career."

He could only stare at her, aghast. "You're serious about this."

"How could I not be?"

"Do you honestly expect me to validate that question with a response? Silence stretched, then transformed into palpable tension. "Yes, there are frustrations when I'm—" he shrugged, at a loss. But then, the words came, in a heartbroken torrent. "I know there are times when I'm on display. When I'm catalogued, and even handled to a degree. But never has it compromised my privacy. Nor would I allow it to compromise yours and Pyper's. And as far as your ex-husband is concerned—" Tyler's tone had turned fierce, his eyes went narrow and angry. "—just let him *try* to interfere with what you and I have together. Just let him *try!* Frankly, I'd love to take him on!"

"That's not within your power to say, Tyler, especially once your fame increases. And you can't stand there and tell me it wouldn't matter!"

"Oh, yes I can." He forced himself to remain calm, but as they faced off, he clutched the edge of the porch railing so hard his fingers hurt. "You matter. Pyper matters. The rest is details, Amy. Insignificant details."

"Insignificant to you. Not to me. To me it's about a sordid divorce. It's about abuse. It's about a degree of alcoholism that ended up devastating not only me, but my daughter as well. My past isn't something I want, or need, to have magnified. A relationship with you would put all of us under intense scrutiny, especially as you gain more and more exposure. And don't discount Mark coming back hunting for money, or Pyper!"

"If that's truly how you feel, then I'll walk away from the career." He spoke with measured calm because he meant the words. With all his heart. "I don't need any of it. What I want is what's been missing in my heart without you, Amy."

"Tyler, that's ridiculous! Please! Listen to me!"

"No, *you* listen to *me*. What I want most in this world is what I've found ever since we reconnected at Woodland. Unless I'm grossly mistaken, you feel the exact same way. When will you learn to trust my feelings enough to just let go, and believe? When will you finally allow this relationship to be everything it was meant to be?"

A tapestry of dreams wove neatly into place: long days and sweet nights with Amy and Pyper, and even more kids down the road. There'd be Christmases, Easter celebrations, music that would fill his house and his heart, tours in the summer, family-friendly life and more than enough love to fill out the remainder of the year. The pictures his heart drew were of a happy, beautiful future—*with Amy*.

"What about all the mistakes I've made?" She eased back against the swing, almost as if she were sinking away from the truth. "What about privacy and protecting Pyper? I pored over everything this morning, and I just can't find the answers."

"You don't need to. What you need to do is stop looking for safety nets, or for assurances and guarantees. There's no such a thing. It won't happen.

Life gives us nothing but God's will and grace, and that's *enough*. You used to know that to the depths of your soul." Tyler took in a fortifying breath. "Nothing will change what life gave either of us, honey. I know Mark left you with a broken heart, but even in your marriage, God stayed with you, and with Pyper. He gave you goodness. Find your way back to that truth and maybe—just maybe—you'll find enough faith to love again."

Her eyes went wide with a kind of marveling wonder. He sensed her longing. In a spot of her heart where he alone was granted entry, he sensed Amy's most strident wishes.

Tyler pushed on. "Life is about change, Amy. We're not meant to remain stationary. I believe God always, *always* meets us where we are in life and can work anything for the good. In the storm of your marriage, your daughter came to life. In the storm of your divorce, God can—and will—continue to work His goodness, love and mercy. Nothing will ever change God, and his absolute goodness, his absolute love for us, because God *alone* is set in stone."

He ignored her glittering tears, her imminent breakdown. He needed her to understand her precious worth, and her hold on his spirit. Desperation poured through his veins, and Tyler hammered his point home. "God shows us pathways—for everything. That encompasses the good and the bad. Evolution is about following His call and that's what life is all about. Live again, Amy. If you don't, you're going to regret it. The loss will be yours. *Again.* Are you willing to accept that?"

"Tyler—" She choked, her eyes wide with desperation and a spirit-deep thirst he only recognized because he felt it so keenly himself.

"No. Hear me out. You're grasping at straws. You're clutching at anything that will justify walking away. Well, you need to ask yourself if walking away from me will save you from heartache." He waited, set his hands on his hips. The words hung in their air, framing the ultimate question that stood between them. His heart teetered precariously when silence held sway.

"Will walking away make you happy? If that's the case, then so be it. I've shown you everything I am, but if that's the case, all I can do now is let you. And yeah, like the fool that I am, I'll keep prayin' you find a way back. I'll keep faith that you'll eventually recognize the connection—the thread our lives have always carried to each other. That's what I'm clinging to, Amy. Not fear. But the decision is yours."

18

Tyler stopped short at the threshold of Amy's room the next morning. He intended to speak with her privately, before they rejoined Pyper downstairs. Next to the bed, Amy's suitcase stood ready, packed and zipped closed.

He hated it.

Not because she was leaving. Leaving he could tolerate. He had expected nothing else at the end of the week. What sliced through him right now was the finality. Unresolved and uncertain, his relationship with Amy was taking an exit right now that he couldn't begin to bear.

She stood at the window, holding back the curtain with her hand, surveying the sprawl of the valley and mountains. Tyler shut out the image of the extended metal pull handle of her luggage and made a decision. He wouldn't let her go without giving her something to think about. And miss.

Without a word, deliberately catching her unprepared, not allowing her a single second to realize his intent and lay out a defense, he pulled her in by the waist and didn't stop until she was pinned against him. His mouth covered hers, his kiss capturing her startled exclamation of surprise and swallowing it up with his own sigh of desire, and surrender.

She melted into him, raking shaky fingertips

through his hair. He clung to her, fed her, adored her, doing his best to seep into the very core of her system until she knew no escape and no other pathway but the one that led to his love.

His fingers dove in as well, combing through her hair, dislodging a satin hair tie. Her hair drifted free around his hands. The familiar smell of his brand of shampoo in her hair, now a fragrant part of the thick, silky strands, caused his muscles to clench with a longing as familiar as his own name, and it broke his aching heart.

They shared so much, yet she could walk away?

The kiss remained intense and heated, spiraling nearly out of control. He barely maintained the wherewithal to pull back and step away from her, refusing the temptation of claiming her definitively, with all the love in his heart.

His body was taut, strung as tight as a wire on one of his six-strings. His breathing was ragged. In slight vindication, though, he realized she suffered as well. So he reigned in his strength and determination. "Amy, think about us. Think about everything you're turning from. I'll be here. I always have been. I feel like it's a huge part of God's plan for me. Know why? Because no other woman comes close to you. I guess it's His will that I let you go again, so I'll do my best to make music my life. I can say this without reservation or anger because I believe in God's promise. He promises that when you love someone well, and when that love is returned, that love will last a lifetime. I look at you, and I know you feel as strongly as I do. I let you go before. I'll let you go again if it'll help you recognize that truth and find your way back to me."

Finished, not letting himself absorb the sheen of

tears that glossed her eyes, or her trembling, kiss-swelled lips and staccato breathing, he took custody of her luggage and carried it downstairs.

Saying goodbye to Pyper was almost as hard.

She was one unhappy young lady, if her flushed face and watery eyes were any indication. When he joined her in the entryway, she slipped off her backpack and charged for him in open trust and love. Tyler took her in, lifting her up and squeezing tight.

He inhaled her sweet scent and feathered his fingers tenderly through her hair. "Miss you already, sugar beet."

"I want to see you soon again," she whispered, her voice shaky.

Convoluted grammar and all, Tyler's heart swelled at the words. "Me, too. But until then, I'll be in touch with you, Pyper." He leaned back, tucking wisps of hair away from her damp, red cheeks. "And here's an idea. I want you to do me a favor."

"What?"

"Every time you see a firefly, I want you to think of me. And I promise, I'll do the same for you."

She nodded, but her chin quivered badly. Tears rolled down her face, and she tucked into his neck and shoulder like a missing puzzle piece. She shook with tears she obviously tried, and failed, to keep silent. Tyler kept rubbing her back, swaying a bit to give them both some semblance of comfort.

For now, though, the airport called. And with every prayer of his heart, he held fast to the belief that releasing his two beautiful doves would ultimately lead them all home, and bring them together once more.

19

For the second day in a row, Amy had a pounding headache.

She'd been back on the job at Edwards Construction for less than a week; the summer schedule for JB's construction company was at an all-time high. She was grateful for busy, fast-passing days. That way, there was far less time to consider the enormous hole in her spirit.

She found herself reliving the parting, that final kiss with Tyler, over and over again. The emotions, the textures and tastes combined to overwhelm her at the most random points during the day. She'd be in the midst of job setups and staffing, service proposals, invoicing—then, in an instant the present world would slip away.

The kiss provided such an exquisite memory—the sensations as real to her now as they were then. She'd lose herself so completely and so willingly to her daydreams, that even her breathing, her heart rate, would react. But then, the return to reality and the recognition of her loss would end her revelry on a note of intense sadness.

Hence the headaches.

Tonight, at least, she had chores at home with which to contend. Pyper dabbled with a spelling game on the computer for a time while Amy retrieved a load of freshly dried laundry from the basement of their apartment unit. Amy had finally started on the photo album for Tyler—the one chronicling his concert at Woodland. After all, it wasn't as if they couldn't remain connected and enjoy each other. Amy figured delivery of the gift might do the job of telegraphing that hope.

For now, however, silence stretched between them, and her heart instantly betrayed the truth that her head couldn't quite grasp yet—she loved him. She ached for him. Friendship, sadly, would never be enough.

The thought plagued her as she returned to her apartment, clothes basket in tow, and went to her bedroom where she intended to sort and fold. Coming upon Pyper caused Amy to stop abruptly, and set aside the laundry basket on the floor next to her bed.

Bathed by the grayish blue illumination of the computer screen, Pyper's entire face looked crumpled. Her lips quaked. Fat tears rolled down her cheeks as she regarded a photograph displayed on the monitor. Tyler. Amy silently cursed herself. She had left the folder of pictures from the Woodland concert open on her task bar. Pyper had apparently clicked away from her game and discovered the readily-available images.

Amy bit the inside of her cheek, going immediately to her shaken daughter. She scooped Pyper up and held on fast. "What's the matter, snug-a-bug?" But she had a feeling she already knew.

"I jus'…I jus' miss him, Mommy. I miss Tyler."

Precisely as she thought. Amy became buried by the weight of that admission. Pyper had come so far— and now, once again, Amy knew she had let her daughter down.

"I can't help it! I wish Tyler was my daddy, and I wish I could see him all the time, and that he could be with me, and you, all the time."

Oh, Lord, help me. Help me now. I can't possibly make it through this without You.

Amy's throbbing head pulsed with a fresh onslaught of pain as she carried Pyper a few feet. In a deliberately playful little tumble, they toppled to the bed, and snuggled up side by side, face to face. Just like they had in Nashville. At Tyler's.

This time it was Amy who reached out and cupped Pyper's cheek. Pyper, in turn, rubbed a soft fingertip against the tight furrow on Amy's forehead.

"I'm so sorry for how sad you feel." Silence followed Amy's apology. "I've messed up a lot, Pyper, but I don't want to hurt you again. Not ever."

Pyper frowned, her eyes still sparkling. "You don't hurt me. You love me. You love me best."

"Oh, honey, you bet I do. The only one who loves you better than me is Jesus. But, still, I wanted better things for you than what you've gotten. I want you to be happy, and to know you're safe, and have a good home, and most of all I want you to know that you're precious, and loved."

Pyper looked into Amy's eyes, her lips rolled inward, pressed between her teeth. The signal was clear—she was emotional, and she was unsettled. But in contradiction to that, she kept a light touch moving against Amy's forehead. Thankfully, Pyper's touch helped ease the relentless band of pressure. Bit by bit, Pyper's eyes dried of tears.

"I know you love me, Mommy, and you made us safe."

"Yeah, but then we had to stay with Ken and

Kiara. We bounced around a lot, didn't we, Pyp?"

"Mm-hmm. They were nice to us. And Annie? She's my bestest friend because we take care of each other and love each other." Pyper blinked her eyes, and smiled. "I think Ken and Kiara and Annie are my family. Like Grandma and Grandpa Maxwell."

A theme developed, swirling slowly into place, but Amy couldn't quite grasp it yet...

"Then I brought you here."

Pyper nodded, and her smile curved larger. "This is *our* house. An' you're not scared of nothin' anymore. You smile. And you and me? We're the *best*. We've got happy."

We've got happy. Amy closed her eyes and took a gulp, thinking, *God, thank you.*

But her daughter wasn't finished yet. Pyper's brows pulled together, and she frowned as tears built once more. "Know what though? You and me never smiled more than when we were with Tyler. I love Tennessee, and I miss him, Mommy. Do you miss him, too? Do you want to see him again? Soon?"

That's when a stunning realization took place. The theme she caught traces of earlier circled to completion and a sharp focus. Not once as Amy poured her heart free, and Pyper examined their lives together, had Pyper reacted in the negative. Pyper transformed every nightmare in their lives into loving kindness, safety, and a fresh, happy life. Together.

We've got happy.

Yes, the past left Pyper sorting through trust and safety issues with adult men, but she worked past them—just like she worked past all the challenges of their life together. Pyper knew the horrors, of course, but she didn't cling to them. By the grace of God alone, she had let them go and continued to embrace each movement forward with hope. Pyper's outlook stayed trained on blessings instead of darkness. Exactly how Amy would want it.

Amy, meanwhile, had worked so hard to make that come to be, she had hardly been aware of, nor acknowledged, the impact of God's hand and the true depth of God's healing, loving power.

With her heart in her throat, she decided to answer Pyper's question, then pose one of her own. "I miss him so very, very much, Pyper. But in order for us to be with Tyler, we'd have to make a whole new bunch of big changes. We'd have to move to Tennessee. It would be far away from everyone and everything we know."

Pyper nodded, and she thought about that for a moment, her lips pursed softly. "Everything 'cept Tyler. And us."

"What about our family?"

"Well. Can they fly like I did? Can we see them that way a lot of times?"

Tyler, Amy imagined, would probably insist on it. "That's a distinct possibility."

Amy's concluding comment caused Pyper to smile, and glow. Amy's heart raced wildly. Energy built so hard and so fast Amy wanted to leap out of bed and start running—clear south to Tennessee. A dam burst free in her heart and love rode in on the energy spill. The right decisions became clearer and clearer, persistent to the point of being undeniable.

We've got happy.

Maybe not yet, Amy thought. Not completely, anyhow—but perhaps soon enough...

∂∞∂

"Kiara...I..." Amy had stalled long enough, and she knew it. She steadied herself. "I need to ask a huge favor."

Amy knelt next to Kiara in the Lucerne's back yard. Together they weeded, not because Kiara had asked, but because Amy had volunteered. It helped Kiara, but it helped Amy as well. Ever since last night, ever since *The Decision*, she had energy to excessive degrees, and she had never, ever been as happy, nor as terrified.

The thoughts crested; not until they receded did she realize Kiara had leaned back on her heels and was watching her. Waiting, and intrigued.

"What's up, Miss Thing?" They shared a smile at the ages-old nickname, but a swell of emotion colored Amy's world. She chewed her lower lip and went back to work pulling away weeds. Kiara, however, didn't continue with their work. "Amy? What's up?"

"Well...I..." Amy focused on their weeding session like a woman on a mission, not meeting Kiara's eyes. "You see...my folks are going to be out of town this coming weekend, and...and...I need to go to Tennessee."

Now Kiara stripped off her gardening gloves and switched from kneeling to sitting cross-legged. "Tennessee."

Amy nodded, and she surrendered the pretense of working. She sat next to Kiara and leaned back, propping against her hands. "I've got a lot to tell you."

Amy launched into a detailed overview of the past week, especially the conversation with Pyper. Kiara listened, silent and intent while Amy let her emotions pour free, especially her growing realization that a life without Tyler wasn't a life lived happily, or in completeness with the call of her heart. Apart from him, she felt apart from God's plan for her life.

"With Mark, I fell in love with an image more than a man. With Tyler, I love the *person*, the boy he was, and the man he's become."

Kiara just nodded, wearing a wise, but non-condemning expression.

"You said it best when he came back into town and you told me to reconcile the boy I knew with the man Tyler is now. I have. Without question. At his core, he was always the one for me. My life and my heart synchronize with him so beautifully. I've been given the most incredible luxury imaginable—the gift of a second chance with the man I should have been with from the start. I'm not turning my back on that again. I can't. To do so is making me miserable."

"OK." Kiara's eyes went wide, and they were misty, but she smiled, and seemed just a touch nostalgic, as though she was already letting Amy go. "You know what I have to ask, right? Just to be a proper big-sister-type person."

Amy laughed. She was already two steps ahead. Reaching into the pocket of her shorts, she pulled out a folded piece of paper and opened it up. "Here witnesseth my reservations at the Country Inn and Suites Hotel in Franklin."

Kiara started to laugh, too.

"Not because I can't be trusted, but because I want you to know exactly where to reach me if anything should come up with Pyper."

"Naturally." Kiara let out a soft sound and pulled Amy in for a long, tight hug. "Oh, Amy...I wonder if you realize how much I'm going to miss you."

"Kiara, c'mon. It's just for the weekend!"

Kiara pulled back. Now the moisture spilled over into a few teardrops that skimmed her cheeks. "Sure it is, Miss Thing. Sure it is."

19

Tyler fiddled restlessly with his cell phone. He held it in his hand and immediately began to drum his fingertips against the side of the device. He paid a visit to his list of contacts and started to scroll until the last name *Maxwell* was highlighted.

She was right there. A simple key click and they'd be connected. He'd hear her voice. Just the idea set his heart racing, his blood pumping.

He backed out of contacts in a hurry, expelling a frustrated groan. The decision had to be hers. But a full week of silence left him less and less able to maintain an even-headed, confident spirit.

He nearly pocketed the unit, but it sprang to life with a vibration, then a chime of melodic bells. It was a ring tone he had assigned to just one person in his far-reaching phone book.

Amy.

He bobbled the phone in his eagerness to activate the connection and see what was going on. What he found wasn't a phone call, but a one-word text message.

Faith.

"What?" Tyler spoke aloud, to the empty quiet of his living room. Was her message sent by mistake? Must be, because it made no sense at all.

This warranted a call. Perfect excuse, Tyler

figured. She had sent the text after all. If it was in error, then she could explain, and maybe talking would open up an avenue to something deeper.

Seconds later, Amy's chimes sounded again. Another text. Another single word.

Opens.

Tyler shook his head, puzzling at the message on the display screen. He wasn't about to try to figure out what was going on. Instead, he called Amy promptly. Four interminable rings later, he got to hear her voice—in recorded form, anyhow.

Hi, you've reached the voicemail for Amy Maxwell. Sorry I missed you, so leave me a message. I'll get back to you. Thanks!

In acute terms, Tyler learned that even in electronic format, the sound of Amy's voice had the power to do him in. He missed her that much. He realized he was hanging on the line, filling up her voicemail with nothing more than dead air so he spoke up in a hurry. "Amy, it's me. Got a couple weird texts and wanted to be sure you're OK, or what it, what they, you know, what you mean." He was reduced to stammering. Tyler rolled his eyes at himself. "Anyway, call me when you get this. Miss you. A lot."

The quietly spoken endnote left him to sigh as he disengaged.

The sound of tires crunching on the gravel drive out front of his home barely registered with Tyler, especially since at that precise moment a third text from Amy rolled in. What in the world was she doing?

Doors.

The doorbell rang and Tyler groaned for a second time. He was so not in the mood for company right now. He strode to the front door, redialing Amy as he yanked it open with an impatient, bothered tug.

Tyler stared, mouth open, phone to his ear. Amy stood before him, the woman he had longed for day in day out, smiling and as glorious as an angel.

Amy held her phone in her hand, and her smile quivered as tears sprang to her eyes. Moisture beaded and glittered on her lashes like diamonds before tracking slowly from the corners of her luminous blue eyes.

"Faith opens doors, Tyler," came her greeting.

He could hardly breathe.

సౌఱ

"Where's Pyper?"

It was the first question that popped into his head and by her smile alone, Tyler knew Amy appreciated that particular consideration.

"She's enjoying a weekend with Annie, and Ken and Kiara."

Tyler still hadn't found center, but that didn't bother him in the least. "Weekend. You're here." He wasn't making much sense, just trying to absorb.

"I'm only here until Sunday. I took the first flight I could after work today and booked the last flight home on Sunday night." She shuffled a bit, seeming, for the first time, a bit uncertain. "That is, if you don't mind."

Mind? Was she insane?

While he stared, Amy looked past his shoulder. "Ah, do you think I could come in, or..."

She burst out laughing, and Tyler joined in. The sound of it filled him like the most beautiful music. Before he let her cross the threshold, he yanked her into his arms and lifted her up, carrying her to the entryway where he spun her in circles.

This was too good to be true! Too blessed for belief!

She was *here*. She was *home*. And she was *his*.

Finally.

It only got better. "I had to see you," she whispered as she flew in his arms. "I had to let you know...know that...that..."

He didn't need roadmaps. He needed Amy. He set her down then pulled her in for a kiss that left them both out of breath and silent with awe.

"I hope you keep selling a lot of records, because my daughter is going to cost you a fortune in family airfare."

"Well, honey, since in the times to come I'd love for her to become *our* daughter, all I can say to that is: bring it on!"

❧✦❧

He made sure he kept his word.

In the months that followed, while summer gave way to the cool breezes and leaf-fire of autumn, Tyler arranged for Amy and Pyper to visit Tennessee as often as possible. Weekends spent together became precious bookends to weeks full of work on the new album, tour plans and preparations, and a relationship with Kellen Rossiter that increased his confidence as each day passed.

September was on the wane when, on a blustery Saturday night, he took them to dinner at The Franklin Chop House, a favorite haunt of theirs. Private booths, intimate atmosphere and delicious food were a perfect combination that allowed them to relax together in peace and anonymity.

Since it was Saturday night, Amy gave voice to her usual weekend-concluding sentiment. "I hate to leave." Tyler kept quiet for the moment and simply watched her instead. Candlelight flickered, shimmering against the curls of her upswept hair as she tilted her head. Her eyes roamed the restaurant and its patrons. "The more time that goes by, the more Tennessee feels like home to me."

Pyper, he noticed, kept watching her mother. The keen-eyed girl sat next to Amy and didn't say a word, but there was expectancy to her appearance. Hope.

That made Tyler smile. "Know what? I forgot something in the car. I'll be right back."

Amy nodded, and opened up the menu to explore dinner options with Pyper. When he passed by, Tyler planted a kiss on Amy's cheek, then Pyper's forehead. His reward? Twin smiles as bright as the twinkle lights that framed in the restaurant ceiling and booth windows.

He returned just a minute or two later, a crackling plastic bag from a local drug store swinging from his hand. He made a ceremonious production out of settling it in the middle of the table. Shocked expressions registered on Amy and Pyper's faces. The waitress approached with her pad in hand. Tyler smiled at her, but shook his head slightly. "Thanks, but can we have a minute here?"

"Absolutely. Y'all just let me know when you're ready."

Amy ignored the exchange. "What's this?"

Tyler stretched back against the padded bench seat and grinned. "Guess there's only one way to find out." With a wave of his hand, he invited her to explore the offering.

"Is it for Mommy?"

"Mmm...actually, sugar beet, it's for all of us."

Pyper bounced in her seat. "Cool! C'mon, Mama, what is it, what is it?"

Amy snickered under her breath and Tyler covered a laugh by coughing. Lately, Pyper seemed determined to pick up a southern twang. She vacillated, currently, between Mommy and Mama, which both Amy and Tyler thought was hilarious. She'd even busted out a "y'all" for the first time yesterday.

Amy unsealed the bag, and her quizzical expression only intensified when she pulled out a good old-fashioned box of sixty-four crayons—secured by a pair of rubber bands.

"This looks like it's for me, Tyler," Pyper said.

"Nope. Not quite. Just wait while your mama opens it."

Amy spread out her hands in surrender, but she smiled. Oh, how she smiled. "I get it. I'm the crayons. You're the rubber bands. Cute reminder of the mission trip to Pennsylvania. But seriously—what's going on?"

Tyler straightened and slid the box toward the place setting in front of him. "Let me explain." He pulled off the rubber bands and knotted them together. After that, he opened the box of crayons so that a vivid, colorful display could be seen and enjoyed. He then settled the offering in front of Amy. "Yes, the rubber bands are me, and I'm connected to you, my lady of rainbow colors and vivid beauty. Kinda like this." Demonstrating, he stretched the slender piece of tan rubber toward Amy. "Here. Take hold. And Pyper, you have a very important job. Make sure she holds on real tight and doesn't let it go no matter what, OK?"

"Mm'kay, Tyler. I will!"

Fascinated, squirming with anticipation, Pyper monitored Amy's hold on the rubber band with the utmost care.

Quick as lightning he removed an item from the pocket of his slacks and hooked it onto the rubber band. He set it gliding along the taut connector where it ended up bumping against Amy's fingers. Pyper gasped. Amy let out a shocked exclamation that nearly caused her to drop her hold on the rubber band, until Pyper yelped. "Hang on, Mama! Hang on tight!"

"Yeah, Amy. Hang on tight," Tyler reiterated tenderly, smiling wide as Amy's stunned eyes touched on his.

Dangling between them, resting against her hand, was a brilliant cut solitaire diamond set in platinum. It sparkled in the dim lighting of the restaurant like wildfire.

"T..T..Tyler..."

"Mommy, it's the prettiest ring ever in the world!"

Tyler gave the little girl a moment to settle. "I can't think of a more perfect moment to ask you to be my wife, Amy. I want Pyper to be my daughter. I want you to grow old with me. I want to build a family with you. You're my best friend, and my soul mate. But beyond anything else, with God's grace and hand, I promise I'll love you forever."

Amy remained silent and overcome, the fingertips of her free hand pressed against her trembling lips. Pyper squiggled, seeming to fight the urge to cut in. In the end, though, the task proved too great. Pyper let out an urgent sound. "Mama, please say yes. Please? *Please?*"

Amy burst out laughing through an onslaught of tears that flowed down her cheeks. Her hold on the rubber band was so shaky it trembled between them, making the ring dance a bit. Tyler moved his hand toward hers, relaxing the tension on the rubber band. He took possession of the ring, and held tight to Amy's left hand. He arched a brow, waiting.

"Yes! Of course my answer is yes!"

Pyper clapped and let out a shout that drew a bit of attention from nearby guests of the restaurant. Tyler stood just far enough to stretch across the length of the table and kiss Amy's lips. They were moist and giving, salted by her tears. He uncurled her ring finger and slid the ring into place. While Amy and Pyper studied its flash and sparkle, Tyler kissed Amy's cheek. "Didn't I promise you this moment would be precious?"

She nodded. "And you've always, always kept your promises. I love you, Tyler. You've made every one of my dreams come true."

"Well, there's a lot more to come, honey. Just wait and see."

Be sure to look for the other books in the Woodland Church Series!

Hearts Surrender, Book 2

Kiara Jordan is a sophisticated modernista, but beneath an engaging personality and super-model looks, her heart hungers, and she longs for deeper meaning in her life.

Ken Lucerne is the charismatic young pastor of Woodland Church; he's adjusting to life as a widower and copes by keeping as busy as possible with his parish and missionary work.

A home-building mission in Pennsylvania brings them together, and forces them to look hard and deep at the relationship they share, and where God means for it to go. Already bound by mutual respect and caring, love dawns, a love that takes them to a life-point neither would have expected.

After all, can a chic, vivacious woman find fulfillment within the quiet, mission-centered life of a clergyman? Can they trust God's hand strongly enough to surrender their hearts to one another...forever?

Hearts Communion, Book 3

Jeremy "JB" Edwards dreams of one thing: Having a loving wife and children of his own. Not a surprising ambition, since he was raised at the heart of a large, tight-knit family.

Monica Kittelski spends her days at Sunny Horizons Daycare Center pouring her heart and faith into other people's children. But Monica harbors one impossible dream: Having children of her own someday.

JB and Monica seem the perfect match, but what will come of their electric, sassy relationship when Jeremy learns of Monica's infertility?

Hopes and reality collide when they must confront the idea of finding God's plan and following His will when a dearest hope is destined to remain unfulfilled.

Can these two loving, passionate hearts survive a communion of dreams and reality?

Haven't read the story that started it all? Be sure to pick up Hearts Crossing, Available now in electronic formats

"How do you feel about God, Collin?"

"I don't."

Collin Edwards, a former parishioner at Woodland Church of Christ, has renounced God without apology, his faith drained away in the face of a tragic loss.

Daveny Montgomery cares deeply about her relationship with God and the community of Woodland. But lately she's been in a rut, longing for something to reignite her spiritual enthusiasm.

A beautification project at Woodland seems the answer for them both. Daveny spearheads the effort and Collin assists—but only with the renovations, and only because he wants to know Daveny better.

Despite his deepening feelings for her, even stepping into the common areas of the church stirs tension and anger.

Can Daveny trust in Collin's fledgling return to faith? And can Collin ever accept the fact that while he turned his back on God, God never turned his back on him?

CPSIA information can be obtained at www.ICGtesting.com
Printed in the USA
BVOW060705150312

285177BV00001B/1/P